MISSION
TO HORATIUS

STAR TREK®

MISSION TO HORATIUS

Authorized edition based
on the popular television series

by Mack Reynolds

illustrated by Sparky Moore

POCKET BOOKS
New York London Toronto Sydney Toyko Singapore

POCKET BOOKS, a division of Simon & Schuster Inc.
1230 Avenue of the Americas, New York, NY 10020

Copyright © 1968 by Paramount Pictures. All Rights Reserved.
Copyright renewed © 1996 by Paramount Pictures

 STAR TREK is a Registered Trademark of
Paramount Pictures.

A VIACOM COMPANY

This book is published by Pocket Books, a division of
Simon & Schuster Inc., under exclusive license from
Paramount Pictures.

ISBN: 0-671-02812-X

This Pocket Books hardcover printing February 1999

10 9 8 7 6 5 4 3 2 1

POCKET and colophon are registered trademarks of
Simon & Schuster Inc.

Printed in the U.S.A.

CONTENTS

PREFACE

So it's 1970, and I'm eight years old and rummaging around in the dusty back shelves of my local used-book store, where I could get—at prices an eight-year-old could afford—such treasures as out-of-date Hardy Boys novels, Tom Swift novels, and even the occasional and much prized novels about Tom Corbett, Space Cadet.

On this day, not noticeably different from many others spent the same way, I ran across a slightly-worse-for-wear copy of a *Star Trek* novel called *Mission to Horatius.*

I had only recently begun to watch *Star Trek* on a regular basis, at six every weekday evening, and was already entranced. Finding a book devoted to Kirk, Spock, and the others was a delight. It was quickly snatched off the shelves, quickly purchased, and even more quickly read, or rather devoured.

It's twenty-eight years later as I write this, and the path this novel started me on finds me in a position to rescue it from the dusty back shelf once again. Presented now in the twentieth anniversary of Pocket Books' *Star Trek* novel line, in as close to the original form as we can make it, this edition of *Star Trek: Mission to Horatius* is dedicated to every *Star Trek* fan who was ever eight years old.

—JOHN ORDOVER
Executive Editor

AN INTRODUCTION

When man first reached out into space, he began slowly, slowly. *Sputnik 1* and *Explorer 1* came first. Then, in less than a year, the first animal, the dog Laika, shortly to be followed by the first human in orbit. And, more quickly, the first spacecraft to carry more than one person, the first crash landing on the moon, the first woman in space, the first spacewalk, the first landing of an unmanned spacecraft and televised shots of the lunar surface. The first this, the first that;

and finally the first successful landing of man on the moon!

Then came the real explosion. Man to the planets. Probes to Mars. Probes to Venus. The first landings on other worlds, the first bases, the first colonies.

And then, seemingly overnight—with the discovery of the space warp, of hyperlight speeds—mankind was suddenly everywhere. Only a century or two earlier he had measured his distances in miles. Suddenly the term "parsec" came into everyday use. A parsec—3.262 times the distance light can travel in a year's time, or 19.2 trillion miles.

The closest star to our own sun is Proxima Centauri, 4.2 light years away, and suddenly it became a neighbor.

The galaxy to which our solar system belongs—sometimes known as the Milky Way—consists of uncounted billions of suns and possibly millions of worlds quite like our own Earth. And it was these that man began to seek out and colonize, as once the explorers sought out, in their simple wooden ships, new islands and continents to settle.

But each new world—even the Class-M planets, which were the most similar to our own—was at least slightly different, and the colonists from Earth found it necessary to adapt to fit the new conditions. By the time the United Federation of Planets began to patrol the galaxy, there was much that was strange.

Of the strange things man finds in space, however, one of the strangest is man himself when he must adapt to new environments. Whole sets of new problems arose. Among these was the need for man to discipline himself in the protection of other life forms and other cultures, other civilizations foreign to his way of life on Earth.

Thus it was that starships such as the United Space Ship *Enterprise* became necessary to survey new sectors of the galaxy, to assist scientific investigations, to stimulate trade between worlds, to prevent conflicts, to pave man's way, and sometimes even to become involved in relatively minor items, such as searching for a lost explorer, prospector, or schoolmistress. . . .

1.
SECRET MISSION

Dr. Leonard McCoy, senior ship's surgeon of the U.S.S. *Enterprise,* stormed from the turbo-lift elevator which opened onto the starship's bridge and glared about. The scene, however, couldn't have been more normal.

Captain Kirk sat musing in his command chair, facing the large bridge viewing screen. Directly in front of him, also facing the screen, sat the navigator, Ensign Chekov, and Helmsman Sulu. In the outer circular elevation behind them, various crewmen and ship's officers stood or sat before their control panels. Immediately to the doctor's right was Communications Officer Uhura, her trim eyebrows a bit high at his precipitate entry. Immediately across from the elevator and behind the captain, Commander Spock, the ship's science officer, sat at his library computer station, also looking mildly surprised at the doctor's obviously upset condition. Mr. Spock, with his long face, his pointed ears, his satanic eyes, never allowed himself to show more than mild surprise; it would have been beneath his dignity as a supposedly emotionless native of the planet Vulcan.

Captain James T. Kirk looked up as the ship's doctor marched toward him. "Yes, Bones?" he said. "Something bothering you?"

Although he had had wide experience in the Starfleet Service, James Kirk was a young man in his early thirties. An Academy graduate, he held the rank of starship captain, the youngest man in the fleet to do so. He prided himself on the fact that he had won his command solely through his own efforts. He was a handsome specimen, with a wide, generous mouth but with the seriousness that the responsibility of his rank demanded. Even his closest intimates, such as Mr. Spock, Dr. McCoy, and the other senior officers of the *Enterprise*, seldom jested with their captain.

Dr. McCoy stood before him now and put his fists on his hips as though in belligerence. "Look here, Jim," he said, "I demand to know where we're going."

The attention of everyone on the command bridge was on him, but he ignored them all as he glowered into Captain Kirk's face.

Kirk looked at him strangely. "Why, Bones?"

"Why! I'll tell you why! This ship has no business being in space! That's why!"

Mr. Spock replied, "To the contrary, Dr. McCoy. The *Enterprise* was built in space and is much too large ever to land."

Dr. McCoy turned his glare in that direction. "You know what I mean, Spock. We should not be on a mission at this time. We should be in orbit around some Starfleet Command Center for a period of rest and reconditioning of the ship. More than half the crew are due for extended leaves. The chief steward tells me that the commissary is shockingly low on supplies. Scotty tells me that his section is in need of various repairs. I want to know where we're going and how much longer we expect to be in deep space."

Captain Kirk shifted in his chair and allowed himself a slight frown. Dr. McCoy was possibly his closest friend and the only man on board who called the captain by his first name.

He said, "I repeat, Bones—why? What is this sudden interest on your part in the performance of this ship's duties—that is, beyond the workings of the medical department?"

The other snapped, "My interests do not extend beyond the medical department, Jim. That's what I'm talking about."

The captain thought about that. He said, "I see what you mean, Bones. Space strain? The confinement syndrome?"

"Worse than that. Head Nurse Chapel has detected the first symptoms of cafard in Yeoman Thomkins."

Captain James Kirk winced.

Helmsman Sulu looked over his shoulder, his alert face dismayed. "Cafard?" he blurted.

"That will be all, Mr. Sulu," Kirk said. He looked over at his science officer. "Mr. Spock, comments?"

Spock said, "Space cafard. Compounded of claustrophobia, ennui—boredom, if you will—and the instinctive dread of a species, born on a planet surface, of living outside its native environment. The instinctive fear of deep space. Formerly the fear of being in free fall, though that seldom applies any longer. A mania that evidently is highly contagious. It is said that in the early days of space travel, cafard could sweep through a ship in a matter of hours, until all on board were raging maniacs, and—"

Captain Kirk said dryly, "I did not require a complete rehashing of the illness, Mr. Spock."

The science officer finished, however. "It does not, of course, apply to Vulcans. Only to the less adjusted and less well balanced humanoid species."

McCoy snorted. "Unhappily, Spock, you're the only Vulcan aboard the *Enterprise*. The rest of us are subject to cafard."

"All right, all right," Kirk said. He looked at Spock again. "The most recent case known?"

"Only last year—on the Space Scout *Westmoreland*. It was found drifting, the whole crew dead. The investigation determined space cafard."

"Dead! Of what?"

"They had killed each other, Captain. Evidently in their madness."

Lieutenant Uhura couldn't refrain from asking, "Killed each other? How?"

Spock looked at the pretty young lieutenant, his face characteristically empty of emotion. "They tore each other apart with their bare hands, Lieutenant."

Uhura closed her eyes in pain and shuddered.

Kirk said in irritation, "The *Westmoreland,* if I recall, Mr. Spock, was a four-manner without artificial gravity and consequently subject to free fall. The

Enterprise is a starship with a crew of four hundred and thirty persons, a gravitational support system so that Earthside conditions are duplicated, ample recreational facilities, and a completely equipped and staffed ship's sick bay. Do you know of any starship class spacecraft that has ever succumbed to cafard?"

Spock said, "No, Captain."

Captain Kirk looked at his ship's doctor. "Well, Bones—comments?"

Dr. McCoy said testily, "There can always be a first. This ship has been on continual patrol for a year —long past the normal period to be spent in deep space. Our supplies are shockingly low."

"We took on supplies at Space Station K-Eight."

"As you well know, Jim, a space station is not a star base. It lacks the facilities. We took on emergency supplies of fuel and basic food. We did not take on new recreational equipment. We did not have shore leave. The officers and crew were not allowed to journey to their home worlds to visit families, wives, husbands, or sweethearts. It was no more than an emergency stop. Our people need fresh air; they need to participate in sports impossible in the confines of the *Enterprise*. They need to look at mountains, lakes, rivers, and oceans, walk city streets, go to shows, restaurants, have a good time. They're normal, flesh-and-blood people,

Jim. They can't spend their whole lives in the confines of a starship. They go stale. Finally they get sick. I'm warning you, Jim. Cafard is the farthest thing from a joke in the medical book."

Captain Kirk's face worked. "I obey orders, Bones. Like any other ship's captain in the Starfleet."

"They're the wrong orders, then!"

"I didn't issue them."

Dr. McCoy demanded, "I still want to know where we're going. How much longer do you expect to be in deep space?"

Kirk said, looking at him evenly, "I don't know."

Even Spock blinked at that.

Captain Kirk looked around the bridge. "All right, now hear this. All of you. I am under verbal orders only. We were scheduled, as you know, to return to Star Base Twelve for the protracted shore leaves, replenishing of ship's supplies, and the repairs that Bones has pointed out have become necessary during the past cruise. While en route we were redirected to Space Station K-Eight to take on emergency supplies. There it was revealed to me that a subspace distress call had been received by Starfleet Command."

McCoy snorted, "But why us? Why not some other ship?"

The captain looked at him. "We were the nearest."

"The distances can't be as great as all that!"

"Evidently they are, Bones."

Dr. McCoy was unhappy and argumentative. "But where are we heading? What was this distress call?"

"I don't know."

All eyes were on him now. On the face of it, this made no sense at all. Spock lifted his satanic eyebrows in question.

Captain Kirk said wearily, "On my desk is a sealed tape. When we reach our immediate destination, NGC four hundred, I am to open it."

It was Spock who worded it for them all. "Very interesting. As everyone knows, NGC four hundred is about as far into the galaxy as the Federation has penetrated. So far as we are concerned, there is nothing beyond."

"There is always something beyond, Mr. Spock. True, neither the United Federation of Planets, the Klington Empire, nor the Romulan Confederation has penetrated into the quadrant beyond NGC four hundred. However, at the present rate of expansion of all three, it cannot be too very long before we do."

The doctor said testily, "If we have to go as far as NGC four hundred before this mysterious mission even begins, there is simply no saying how much time will be involved. I repeat, I demand that we turn back."

Captain Kirk looked at him for a long, empty moment before answering. Then he said, "Dr. McCoy, the *Enterprise* has a proud tradition. Since I took over its command from Captain Pike, it has never failed to take any assignment ordered, no matter what excuses might be available. I have no intention, Doctor, of ending that proud tradition now."

The glare had returned to the ship doctor's eye. "Very well," he snapped. "But I request that my position be logged."

Kirk looked at him in surprise. He shrugged. "That is your right, Doctor."

He reached forward, touched a switch, and then said in a flat tone, "Captain's log, star date"—he cast his eyes up at the chronometer-calendar on the bulkhead —"three-four-seven-five, point three. We are on a secret mission, the nature of which will not be revealed to us until we have reached the position NGC four hundred. Senior Ship's Surgeon Leonard McCoy has officially put himself on record as opposed to continuing on the grounds that the personnel of the *Enterprise* are in no condition to remain in space."

Captain Kirk flicked the switch again, ending his log entry, and turned back to the doctor. "Bones," he said, "I will make one concession to your fears. We'll speed up as much as possible."

He flicked another switch and looked up into the intercom viewing screen which faded in on an empty command chair in the engineering section.

Kirk said crisply, "Lieutenant Commander Scott, please."

The screen faded again and then flicked to a smaller compartment which was a maze of electronic equipment. Three men in coveralls were working over a confusion of wires, tubes, and circuits.

Senior Engineering Officer Montgomery Scott, an electronic wrench in one hand, a tiny power connector in the other, looked up impatiently until he saw who it was. Then he came to his feet and looked into the screen.

"Aye, Captain?" He said over his shoulder to his two engineers, "Bide a wee, lads."

Kirk said, "Scotty, we've been proceeding at a standard warp factor five. Please increase this to warp factor seven."

"Seven?" The chief engineer scowled.

"That is correct." Kirk began to extend his hand to flick off the intercom.

"Wait a minute, sir," Scott said worriedly.

"What is it, Scotty?"

"An order's an order, sir, and if necessary, of course. . . ." He hesitated.

Captain Kirk could see that the craggy-featured space engineer was unhappy. He well knew the other's fierce pride in the engine department of the ship. And he also knew how much the Scotsman hated to admit that anything in his department wasn't functioning at top level.

Kirk said, "Well? What is it, Scotty?"

Scott took a deep breath. His voice was almost surly. "Captain, we've been on continuous patrol for a solar year, and . . . well, sir, I hate to push the engines beyond our present speed." The Scottish burr in the engineer's voice was obvious, as it always was when he was under pressure.

Kirk stared at him. "We've been proceeding at warp five, Scotty. I fully realize that maximum safe speed of this vessel is warp six, but that it is capable of warp eight, under considerable strain. Do you mean to tell me—"

The senior engineering officer said doggedly, "You are the captain, sir. I'll give you warp six, if you feel it necessary. However, any warp factor beyond that is against my better judgment."

"We're in a hurry, Scotty."

"Aye, sir. Obviously. However, if you order me to proceed at a factor greater than warp six, it is over my protest, considering the present condition of the

23

outboard engine nacelles, both of which need replacing."

"Your protest, Scotty?"

Scott said doggedly, "If one of the matter anti-matter engines blows this far out, we'd take the rest of eternity to limp back on the impulse power engines. In fact, we'd have to send out a distress call for emergency repairs. It'd be a spot on my record I wouldn't like to see, Captain Kirk."

"Very well, Scotty," Kirk said stiffly. "We'll proceed at warp factor six." He flicked off the screen.

Dr. McCoy had gone over to Spock's library computer station where he was saying, "You have some influence over him, Spock. Use it to have him turn back."

Spock said, "My dear doctor, he is the captain. Besides, I am as familiar with the *Enterprise's* proud tradition as anyone else. Most enviable. I would dislike to see it ended by a simple fear of the crew's going stale."

The doctor stared at him. "Going stale!" he blurted. "Spock, you have no conception of the reality of cafard." He turned to stomp off in disgust.

Captain Kirk, still irritated, was staring at the helmsman before him. He said suddenly, "Mr. Sulu, what in the world is wrong with your tunic?"

The helmsman turned, his face blank. "My tunic, sir?"

"That bulge. It seems to be moving."

Lieutenant Sulu cleared his throat unhappily. "Bulge, sir?"

Captain Kirk said, *"Mr.* Sulu, what do you have there under your tunic?"

By this time all attention was on the slightly built helmsman, even that of the disgruntled Dr. McCoy.

Sulu closed his eyes in apprehension. "Well, sir," he said, "it's probably Mickey."

The captain looked at him.

Sulu cleared his throat again and reached a hand up under his uniform tunic. He brought forth a small brown animal. He set it down on the console before him and said apologetically, "Mickey, sir."

Captain Kirk stared. "Where did *that* come from, and what is it doing on my bridge?"

Sulu said, more bravely now but still with the element of apology in his voice, "From the planet Vishnu, sir. When we stopped at Space Station K-Eight I was fortunate enough to acquire Mickey from one of the locals. He's a highly trained animal, sir."

"I thought you were clear on the orders against pets aboard the *Enterprise* since our troubles with the

25

tribbles, Lieutenant." The captain was looking with distaste at the little beast, which was nervously twitching its well-whiskered nose and staring back at the ship's skipper with slightly reddish eyes.

"Well, yes, sir, of course. However, Mickey isn't exactly a pet, sir."

"Not a pet? What would you call him, or *it,* then? I assume, Lieutenant, you didn't bring it aboard with the intention of utilizing it as food."

"Eat Mickey? Oh, no, sir. He's the first of my collection of exotic animals, Captain. You see"—the words were beginning to come in an enthusiastic rush now—"here we are, touching a hundred different planets, many of them with strange life forms. The way I see it, we should pick up samples of these and when we return to Earth turn them over to the zoological authorities. Very educational, sir. Perhaps someday—" there was a wistful something in Sulu's voice now—"someday, perhaps, there will be a section of a zoo back on Earth called the Lieutenant Sulu section, consisting entirely of rare animals I have donated."

Spock had been eyeing the crouching little animal. He said now, "Most interesting. I had thought them extinct."

The captain looked at him. "Mr. Spock, comments?"

Spock said, "If Lieutenant Sulu wishes to start a collection of exotic alien life forms, I would suggest he begin with other than, ah, Mickey. We have a specimen here of *Rattus norvegicus* of the family *Muridae*, originally native to Central Asia—"

"A bit less technical, if you please, Mr. Spock."

"Better known as the brown rat. If I am not mistaken—"

"You are seldom mistaken, I find, Mr. Spock," the captain said dryly.

"—the brown rat migrated westward early in the eighteenth century, reaching Great Britain about A.D. 1730. A great frequenter of ships, it had soon spread throughout the world, reaching the United States in 1775."

"Very well, Mr. Spock, we will not at this time go into the full details of the rodent family." The captain looked at his chief helmsman witheringly. "I doubt if the zoo authorities back on Earth would be interested in your far-traveled specimen, Mr. Sulu. Consequently—"

Dr. McCoy spoke up. "Jim, I suggest you allow Lieutenant Sulu to retain his trained pet as a ship's mascot. We can use such little diversions. Our recreational facilities are in a sad state after all these months in deep space."

Captain Kirk was not averse to placating his old friend, whom he had just had to step upon. He said, "Very well. However, I am not interested in having, ah, Mickey, on my bridge during your watch, Mr. Sulu. I suggest that you take him below. Mr. Akrumba, please take over Mr. Sulu's position at the helm."

"Yes, sir." The large junior officer stepped forward and slid into the chair Sulu vacated.

The navigator spoke up. "Sir, we have reached our position. NGC four hundred."

Dr. McCoy snorted. "So now, I assume, we can find out just what this mysterious mission is and how long we can be expected to remain in deep space."

2.
MYSTERY
PLUS MYSTERY

Captain Kirk said, "Mr. Chekov, go to my quarters. On my desk you will find a tape. Please bring it here."

"Yes, sir." The ensign made his way toward the turbo-lift elevator, the door of which slid open at his approach and closed automatically behind him.

Those remaining behind on the bridge waited it out.

The captain flicked an intercom switch and said, "Mr. Scott, we have arrived at our destination. We will drop out of space warp and remain at these coordinates until further orders are determined."

Scott's voice came through. "Aye, sir."

Chekov returned, having obviously made every effort at speed. He laid the message container before his commanding officer and stepped back, his youthful Slavic face as inquisitive as any of the others on the ship's bridge.

The captain broke the seal on the container, brought forth the tape, and inserted it deftly in a scanner which he then activated. He stared down into the screen and almost immediately scowled.

"The sun system Horatius," he said, looking up. "Mr. Spock?"

The Vulcan raised his strangely shaped eyebrows. "I do not believe I have ever heard of it, Captain."

"Which surprises me, Mr. Spock. Horatius. I can't even think of the source of the name."

The science officer was on firmer ground now. "A legendary Roman hero, sir. The story is that when the Etruscans, under Lars Porsena, were attempting to capture Rome, there was only a single bridge crossing the Tiber River, and the Etruscans were advancing rapidly. The sole chance was to cut the bridge down before the enemy could overrun it. Horatius and two companions—"

"Just a minute, Mr. Spock," the captain broke in. "We will take your word for it."

The captain returned to the perusal of his orders. He looked up at last, his face very thoughtful. "Our instructions, briefly, are to proceed to the star system Horatius and investigate the subspace distress call received by Starfleet Command."

"Who issued the distress signal, Captain?" Spock asked.

Kirk frowned. "It was evidently cut off before that was revealed. However, the call came through in Earth Basic, which would indicate a planet settled by humans. Please check the computer banks, Mr. Spock."

Spock bent over his library computer station, peering into the hooded screen, muttering orders, occasionally flicking controls.

In a surprisingly short period of time, he raised his head, his face registering uncharacteristic amazement. "Very interesting," he said.

"I am sure, Mr. Spock," the captain said dryly. "But will you let us in on your newfound knowledge?"

"It would seem, Captain, that there is very little information in the computer banks on the Horatian system. It is at the very extreme of this quadrant. Its very discovery, in the early days of space travel, was an accident. A small freighter inadvertently fell out of space warp and into under-space. When its crew managed to force the ship back into warp, it materialized near Horatius and set down on one of the three Class-M planets which orbit the sun."

"Three?" Kirk said.

"Yes, sir. Later they were named Neolithia, Mythra, and Bavarya. But to resume. The space freighter was forced to remain until the necessary repairs were made. The star was reported and charted, but since it remained in such a far sector, in a direction not being exploited by the Federation, it was largely ignored."

Captain Kirk was scowling. "But a distress signal in Earth Basic has come from there."

"Yes, sir. Evidently, although the Federation has not reached out to that point, human colonists have. In fact, the Horatian star system was settled by people who wished to avoid contact with the Federation."

"But why?" Lieutenant Uhura asked.

Spock looked at the dark-complexioned communications officer. "The information is sketchy, Lieutenant, but it would seem that the colonists of the Horatian system are not in sympathy with Federation ways and have fled to such a distant sector to escape them."

All present were looking at him blankly.

Dr. McCoy snorted. "Why? Are they insane?"

Spock shrugged and looked back briefly into the

hooded screen. "The group that first settled and named their planet Neolithia evidently wished to return to nature and abandon the highly technical civilization that exists on the Federation worlds. The second group seemed somewhat similar to the Pilgrims who settled New England; that is, they wished to find a place where they could worship without interference."

Captain Kirk said, "That's nonsense. There are no restrictions on religious matters in the Federation. Why, General Order Number One specifically states that no starship shall interfere with the political, economic, or religious systems of any world."

Spock said, "However, Captain, suppose the religion was that of Baal?"

"I am afraid that my studies of comparative religion are not quite as wide as yours, Mr. Spock. And once again I must mention that you continue to amaze me with your knowledge of the small planet of my birth. Who was Baal?"

"The chief god of the Phoenicians, Captain. His followers were obligated to throw their first-born child into the flaming maw of Baal as a human sacrifice."

Uhura, ever sensitive, closed her eyes as if in pain.

"Go ahead, Mr. Spock," the captain said impatiently. "That accounts for two of the planets. And the third?"

Spock glanced back into the hooded screen of his

library computer and frowned. "Bavarya. The most recently settled of all. Evidently only half a century or so ago. A thousand colonists, no more. Political nonconformists. And that is practically all we know of them."

Dr. McCoy said, "Why all the secrecy? Why all the nonsense of waiting until we reached this point before disclosing the orders?"

The captain had been looking back into his tape scanner. "That is at least partially explained, Bones. Although not members of the Federation, all three of the Horatian planets were colonized by Earthlings, and thus we have a moral obligation. However, Starfleet Command is not as yet ready to expand in this direction and is aware of the fact that if either the Romulan Confederation or the Klington Empire *thought* we were doing so, they might hurry their own exploration. This whole expedition is top secret, and very few persons even at Starfleet Command know that we are on our way."

He turned and spoke to the navigator. "What is the listing for the Horatian group on the star chart of this quadrant?"

"The system is NGC four-three-four, sir."

"Very well. Mr. Akrumba, lay a course for NGC four-three-four. Warp factor six."

"Aye, aye, sir. Bearing of thirty-seven, mark two-eleven, sir."

"Very well, Mr. Akrumba."

Dr. McCoy growled, "Months!"

Approximately a dozen off-watch personnel were sprawled lethargically about the wardroom. Four of them were playing cards, some were reading, and a couple were playing chess. The rest were slumped in chairs, talking a bit, but largely staring blankly at nothing in particular.

Lieutenant De Paul threw his cards to the table in disgust. "That's it," he snarled. "No more canasta for me. What kind of a game is it when Dick, here, sits next to me and draws six wild cards to my one? What good is a game that's nine-tenths luck?"

One of the others protested. "It's one of the few games left that we're not sick and tired of."

"Ha!" De Paul snorted. "You can add it to the list, as far as I'm concerned. What do you say we go back to poker?"

"Poker?" Ensign Chekov grunted. "What good is poker if you can't bet? And you know the regulations against gambling in space."

"How about looking at some Tri-Di shows?" somebody suggested listlessly.

Security Officer Masaryk growled, "Tri-Di shows? You won't have to show them. I can describe every one on board by heart. I've seen them fifty times over."

Lieutenant De Paul said, "Somebody hand me that tape, *1001 Popular Games Down Through the Centuries*. We've got to kill time someway." He slapped the tape into a scanner, but nobody seemed very hopeful that he would come up with anything.

Lieutenant Uhura, who had been softly strumming on her specially made five-string guitar on the other side of the compartment, said softly, "I read once that killing time isn't murder. It's suicide."

Chekov snorted. "You don't kill time on the *Enterprise* these days. It dies a slow death from boredom."

De Paul, scanning the taped book, said, "Gin rummy. Did we ever play gin rummy?"

"On the cruise before last," somebody groaned. "We played it until it ran out of our ears. I'm as tired of that as you are of canasta."

Lieutenant Chang called over to Uhura, "How about a song? There ought to be something to cheer us up."

Everyone seemed in favor of that.

Uhura smiled as she strummed louder, and a soft, faraway gentleness came into her eyes. She began an age-old folk song.

One of the guitar strings went *ping*.

"Oh, good heavens," she complained. "That's my last spare." She twisted her lovely mouth into a *moue*. "And Commander Scott tells me that we're so low on some materials that he won't be able to manufacture new ones for me. Well, dear children, from now on any music from this box is played on four strings."

"Oh, great," somebody muttered.

"I think I'll read awhile," Ensign Freeman said lackadaisically.

"Read?" De Paul said. "Read what? We've all read everything in the recreational library three times over. It hasn't been replenished for well over a year. And I simply don't have the gumption these days to wade through technical books the way the chief engineer seems to be able to."

Science Officer Spock left the elevator and hurried over to his position at the library computer station. A planet loomed in the large bridge viewing screen.

Captain Kirk, already in his command chair, said to his first officer, "The planet Neolithia, Mr. Spock."

"Yes, sir." Spock took his chair and began throwing switches, touching controls.

Captain Kirk said, "Mr. Sulu, go into standard orbit, please. Twenty-thousand-mile perigee."

"Aye, aye, sir."

Kirk said, "Lieutenant Uhura, open the hailing frequencies."

"Aye, aye, sir."

Sulu said, "Standard orbit, sir. Twenty-thousand-mile perigee."

"Thank you, Mr. Sulu. Lieutenant Uhura?"

"No response, sir. Sir. . . ."

The captain looked at her. "Yes?"

"Captain, there seem to be no radio emanations whatsoever."

Kirk scowled and looked at the navigator. "This *is* the planet Neolithia?"

"Yes, sir. That is, if the scanty information we have on the Horatian system is correct, sir."

"Mr. Spock, your sensors on this, please."

"Yes, sir." Spock's long, agile fingers raced. Shortly the Vulcan's face registered rare surprise. "Most unusual," he muttered. He touched other controls.

"Well, Mr. Spock?"

Spock turned to his commanding officer. "Sir, it would seem that not only is the planet below completely lacking any radio emanations whatsoever, but it has never had them."

"Don't be ridiculous, Mr. Spock. Neolithia is settled by human colonists."

Spock said nothing.

The captain, scowling, flicked a screen control. The screen increased magnification many times, until the view was as clear as if the *Enterprise* hovered no more than a mile or so above the surface.

The scene couldn't have appeared more Earthlike. But it was as an Earth of centuries past. It could have been, perhaps, Kansas in an age before the white man made his appearance—indeed, before the Indians had acquired horses and thus achieved the ability to pursue the vast herds of buffalo, elk, deer, and antelope. There were no signs of human habitation—neither cities, towns, villages, nor the smallest of hamlets.

"Mr. Spock, atmosphere analysis?"

Spock said slowly, "Captain, most unusual. The atmosphere is Earthlike. Nitrogen, oxygen, with traces of argon, krypton, and neon. Temperature seventy-five degrees Fahrenheit. Gravitational force identical to that of Earth. However, Captain, the sensors detect one oddity."

"Well, Spock?"

The science officer looked at him strangely. "Sir, there are no signs of . . . of what was once called smog. No traces of man-made industrial fumes, the burning of fossil fuels such as coal and oil."

"What are you suggesting, Mr. Spock?"

"This planet is not inhabited by mankind, Captain."

"You are jumping to conclusions. Radiation? Perhaps their civilization utilizes nuclear power."

"None whatsoever, Captain. And had they—ever—there would be at least traces in the atmosphere."

The captain's eyes went back to the viewing screen. He touched controls and swept over a larger area. The scene below changed little, though for the next fifteen minutes they scanned plains, lakes, rivers, mountains.

"Are you suggesting," Kirk finally snapped at his first officer, "that the colony has been wiped out?"

"I would not know, sir," Spock said simply. "But as you see, there are no signs below of destruction such as would necessarily result from wholesale devastation."

The captain came to a snap decision and rose to his feet.

"Mr. Sulu, have the transporter room stand by, and prepare to accompany us. Mr. Spock, you, Ensign Chekov, Yeoman Doris Atkins, and—"

Dr. McCoy had entered toward the end of the conversation. He said, "Ah, Jim. . . ."

The captain looked at him. "Yes, Bones? I had intended you to accompany us, but you seemed so wrapped up in your pursuit of space cafard symptoms that I thought you wouldn't feel you could be spared."

"Yes, Jim," the doctor said testily. "However, I was about to suggest that you limit your group to five

41

persons and take along a specimen container. In view of the, ah, mysterious qualities of this supposedly inhabited planet, perhaps it would be well if Mr. Spock could return to the ship with some local flora and fauna as well as soil and mineral specimens. Analysis might indicate what has happened to the original colonists."

"Your point's well taken, Bones. Mr. Spock?"

"Very good, Captain. I'll arrange for the container."

3.
BACK TO THE STONE AGE

CAPTAIN JAMES KIRK entered the transporter room, buckling on the weapons belt from which his phaser pistol hung. The others had already gathered. The transporter officer stood at the freestanding console, a technician next to him. On the circular platform of the transporter chamber itself, a large specimen box already stood on one of the six light panels.

Kirk looked at his second-in-command. "Well, Spock, any opinions on where to touch down?"

"An interesting question, Captain." The Vulcan looked down at his own phaser pistol. "General Order Number One restrains us from using our sophisticated weapons against advanced life forms, though it does not prohibit us from protecting ourselves against carnivora and such. However, it would seem unfortunate if we should materialize in the midst of one of those numerous herds of herbivorous animals—both for them and for ourselves. In scanning tapes of the America of the so-called Old West, I have sometimes pondered the question of whether a regiment of, say, the Civil War period, could have withstood a stampede of a bison— ah, buffalo, I believe they called them—herd numbering perhaps a million head."

"Could we have your opinion, Mr. Spock, without a dissertation on early American history?" the captain said dryly, giving his phaser holster a final adjusting pat.

"It would seem to me, Captain, that we had better set down in a hilly, more barren spot, where we would be less apt to be trampled to death before even our phasers were able to decimate the large animals that seem to graze on Neolithia."

Kirk grunted a laugh. "You're obviously right, Spock." He looked at the transporter officer. "Otherwise there would seem to be little choice."

"Yes, sir." The other peered into his screen and made adjustments.

The captain, Spock, Sulu, the yeoman carrying her portable sensor-computer-recorder slung over her shoulder, and Ensign Chekov mounted to their light panels. Chekov loosened his phaser in its holster, in readiness for a possible quick draw.

Kirk said to the transporter officer, "Very well, mister."

The other snapped a quick command to the technician, who dropped levers and threw the activating switch. A column of light gleamed above each transport panel, and the group faded, became transparent, and disappeared.

They materialized in a small glade with wooded hills to each side, except one which enjoyed a stream of exceedingly clear water.

Ensign Chekov, ever security conscious, kept his hand a few inches from his phaser pistol; his eyes darted about. The others stood in open admiration, surveying the countryside.

Even Spock was able to say, "Actually, most fascinating. I have visited Earth but seldom; however, this would seem almost a duplicate of the planet before the advent of technology."

Sulu, in a hushed voice, asked, "Have you ever been

in the national park of Kyoto?"

Captain Kirk said, "Mr. Sulu, I have never even been in Japan, though I appreciate your esthetic reaction. Nevertheless, I suggest we postpone appreciation of Neolithia's scenic beauties and proceed to our task of discovering why this supposedly colonized planet is—"

He was interrupted by a scream that temporarily froze them all, save possibly Spock, and then broke into a sound that could only be described as a doglike barking.

From a clump of trees across the glen there erupted a savage figure, mounted upon a horselike quadruped and charging toward them at breakneck speed. The distance was but a few score yards.

Yeoman Doris Atkins, veteran though she was, resorted to an instinct reaching back into the mists of antiquity. She gave a very feminine squeal.

Sulu yelped, "Hey, look out!"

Spock's eyebrows went up.

Ensign Chekov went into a gunman's crouch and his hand blurred into motion.

Captain James Kirk took a quick step forward and threw up Chekov's gun hand so that the bolt burned blue into the sky. Then he pushed his junior officer to one side and to the ground, even as the rider was

upon them. He threw himself to the other side, but not quickly enough to prevent the fur-clad rider, his face a mask of unbelievable color, from striking out at him.

The savage screamed, "Coup!" and slashed with what seemed to be a riding crop.

The blow caught the stumbling James Kirk across the cheek, raising an immediate welt. And then the rider was past them and heading for the forest beyond, crouched low over his horse's neck and shouting back his barklike war cry.

Chekov was up on one knee, his phaser again at the ready, but his eyes, bewildered, were on his commanding officer.

Kirk, his eyes narrow, snapped, "Mr. Chekov, throw your side arm on stun effect and bring that fellow down!"

The savage was almost to the trees, still barking his triumph. Ensign Chekov brought up his phaser pistol and fired immediately when the weapon reached eye level.

"Good shot!" Sulu yelped in approval.

The savage tumbled from his seat to the ground and remained motionless. Spock, Sulu, and Yeoman Atkins headed for him.

Kirk paused long enough, however, to look at Ensign

Chekov. He said, "Mister, if I hadn't thrown up your gun hand, you would undoubtedly have killed him. I suggest that upon our return to the *Enterprise* you review General Order Number One. We have landed upon a planet colonized by mankind, without, I might add, even so much as an invitation from the authorities, whoever they may be. The repercussions, were we to butcher any of the citizens, would reach all the way back to Starfleet Command."

"Yes, sir," Chekov said. "It seemed to me as though the man were attempting to kill us."

"You should have looked closer, mister." Captain Kirk followed the others. "In the first place, you could hardly call the lad a man."

Chekov was taken aback as he stared down at the crumpled figure. Jim Kirk was obviously right. This was no more than a teen-age boy, clad in primitive furs, his face painted grotesquely.

Spock's eyebrows were high.

Kirk said, "Comments, Mr. Spock?"

"Most interesting, Captain. The boy is obviously an Earthling. He is made up in war paint in the fashion of primitives. His armament seems to consist of nothing save a short stick. I submit, Captain, that in the early Indian days, it was considered a greater honor on the part of a warrior to strike an enemy with a stick and

49

'count coup' upon him, as the term went, than to kill him."

The captain grunted. "Mr. Sulu, Mr. Chekov, keep a keen watch. Possibly this ambitious youngster has companions. If they see him like this they will assume him dead, and we have no reason to believe they haven't weapons more potent than sticks."

Chekov and Sulu drew their phasers.

Kirk went on. "Yeoman, your tricorder, if you please. Do the sensors record any sign of intelligent life in the vicinity?"

Yeoman Doris Atkins activated the large, rectangular, handbag-like device she had slung over her shoulder. After a brief moment she shook her head. "No, sir. Some lower life forms, including the, uh, horse that seems to have stopped about a quarter kilometer ahead. But no indication of intelligent life except us in this clearing."

"Mr. Spock, see what you can do about reviving the boy."

The Vulcan bent down, and only his superior reflexes avoided the sudden snap of teeth in the direction of his outstretched hand. He jerked it back and came erect.

"It would seem that would be unnecessary, Captain."

The fur-clad Neolithian sat erect and glared defi-

50

antly at the Federation representatives grouped around him.

"I am Grang of the Wolf clan and have no fear of death!"

He spoke in a most passable Earth Basic, but in spite of the bravery of his words there was a slight tremor in his voice.

Captain Kirk said dryly, "And I am James of the Kirk clan and have only the usual, normal dread of death. So we seem to be even, boy. But why the attack upon us?"

"Had I been a full warrior and armed with bow or spear I would have slain you all."

"Well, thank goodness for small favors," Sulu said sourly.

The captain said, "That will be all, Mr. Sulu. At least the lad has courage." He turned back to the fallen young savage. "But why did you feel it necessary to attack us, ah, Grang? We have done you no harm, and, in fact, we have come to help you—assuming that this is where the distress call came from."

"Help us?" The boy, seeing that evidently they had no immediate plans to harm him further, came to his feet and glared at the others. "You have come to kill us or capture us and fly us away in your iron birds from the sky."

Inadvertently Kirk cast his eyes upward. However, the *Enterprise*'s orbit was too high for the starship to be visible from this point.

Spock murmured, "Most interesting."

Kirk looked at him. "Your opinion, Mr. Spock?"

"Since Grang, here, cannot have observed the *Enterprise,* Captain, he manifestly must be referring to raiders from some other spacecraft."

"Why spacecraft? Why not local aircraft?"

"You forget, Captain, that our sensors were able to detect no emanations that indicated technology on Neolithia of the order that could produce airplanes, even primitive ones."

"You're right, of course," the captain admitted. He looked at the boy musingly.

The Neolithian was almost full-grown. In fact, his stature was about that of Sulu, the shortest of the *Enterprise* group. His figure was straight and lithe, and his features were open and clear-cut, to the extent they could be made out through the heavy war paint. He hid the apprehension he must have felt and stared back at his captors defiantly.

Kirk said gently, "Son. . . ."

"I am not your son. We are not even kin. I am of the Wolf clan and—"

"All right, all right. Listen, Grang, we have no

desire to harm you. However, we would like to speak to your authorities. We are on a mission of assistance and have no desire to kill or capture your people."

The boy was obviously disbelieving, but he said, "Authorities?"

Spock put in, "Your chiefs, your headmen, your elders. . . ."

Understanding dawned. "You mean the Council of Patriarchs?"

"Exactly," Kirk said. "Now, if you will lead us. . . . Certainly they can't be too far away"—he frowned—"in spite of the fact that the ship's sensors seemed not to have detected them."

"They will kill you all," Grang said defiantly. However, it was obvious the youngster was rapidly losing his original fear of these strangers.

Chekov cleared his throat wryly.

Captain Kirk said, "In which case you will have served your, ah, clan, by delivering us up to them, Grang."

The boy thought about it. "Very well, I will lead you. You will all be killed by our warriors in vengeance for those you have kidnapped and killed in your many raids."

"Things are bad everywhere," Sulu muttered. However, he grinned at the boy, whose courage was obvious.

53

The young savage turned and began to walk in the direction his horselike animal had taken.

Captain Kirk called, "Just a minute." He brought his communicator from his tunic and flicked erect the antenna grid. He said, "Kirk to *Enterprise.*"

"Lieutenant Uhura here, Captain," a voice came back.

Kirk said into the communicator, "Please instruct Commander Scott to assume my command chair and to keep a fix on us. There are some developments here we plan to explore."

"Aye, aye, sir."

Kirk flicked the antenna grid down and returned the device to his tunic.

"All right," he said. "Let's go. Grang, show us the way. Mr. Spock, follow immediately behind me. Keep your tricorder activated, tuned to detection of intelligent life. Yeoman, you follow Mr. Spock. Mr. Sulu, Mr. Chekov, bring up the rear, your phasers on stun effect. Remember, all of you, arrows and spears are quite as effective as the most advanced weapons, so far as terminating life is concerned, *if* they are given the chance to be used."

"Yes, sir." Chekov spoke as if his mouth were dry.

They followed the youth, who proceeded down a

forest path. After a quarter kilometer they came upon Grang's animal, which was grazing quietly. Grang whistled softly to the beast, which immediately came to him.

Kirk said, "You're free to go, if you wish, but we're anxious to meet this Council of Patriarchs of yours, and surely our numbers are such that your clan need not fear us."

"The clan Wolf fears nothing," Grang said strongly, taking up his animal's reins, but making no attempt to mount.

"I'm beginning to believe him," Sulu muttered.

Kirk said, "All right, Grang, continue."

They approached a lofty cliff, which the narrow path skirted, and proceeded possibly another quarter kilometer before rounding a bend and pulling up abruptly. There before them loomed a large cave entrance. Grang turned defiantly.

"The cavern of the Wolf clan," he said proudly. "Now all of you will be slain by our warriors."

"Oh, fine," Sulu muttered. "I can hardly wait."

Ensign Chekov said in amazement, "You mean your whole clan, or tribe, or whatever you call it, lives in this cave?"

Kirk said, "Mr. Spock, your sensors?"

The Vulcan shook his head. "Still no indication of

human life, Captain. However, there is an interesting aspect."

"Well?"

"Within the vicinity there is a considerable radioactive element. If I were on the ship and had at hand the resources of the library computer. . . ."

"For the time, we will proceed, Mr. Spock. Perhaps later we can go into the broader aspects of the problems that present themselves here." He turned to the young savage. "Grang?"

In the past half hour the boy had lost some of his belligerence, since these strangers had not harmed him. In fact, he was obviously intrigued by them, their equipment, and the mystery of from whence they had come. He hesitated.

"If I take you inside, you will be slain by the warriors."

Kirk said, "A chance we'll have to take, Grang. I have already told you we wish you and your people no harm. Perhaps I can convince your patriarchs of that fact."

Yeoman Doris Atkins winked at the boy. He blinked, taken aback by her smile. "We'll be all right," she said. "Don't worry about us."

That seemed to set him back still further. It had evidently come to him that he *was* a bit apprehensive about these new companions of his coming to an unfortunate end. Other than their early scuffle, they had offered him nothing but kindness.

Frowning, he turned and resumed leading them into the wide mouth of the cave.

Large as the opening was, the group from the *Enterprise* were still astonished by the tremendous size of the interior. Indeed, the mammoth cavern towered so high above them that the ceiling seemed to fade into the distance. The interior stretched back as far as the eye could see. Strangest of all was the almost phosphorescent quality of the rock of the walls and ceiling, so that, though dim, the cavern's interior was not truly dark. It was certainly light enough so that one could make his way without tripping.

For a moment they stood immediately inside the entrance and peered before them in an attempt to accustom their eyes to the dim light.

Kirk said, "Mr. Spock, your sensors?"

"Astonishing, Captain. They seem to fail to function."

"Yeoman?"

"And mine, Captain," Doris Atkins said in puzzlement.

"Evidently we find why the ship's sensors were unable to detect life. The radioactive qualities present must blanket the sensors." The captain looked at their guide. "You mean your people are able to live in this atmosphere?"

"We have done so," Grang said, his voice slightly surly, "ever since the raiders began to kill and capture us."

Spock said, "You must realize, Captain, that all radioactive elements are not necessarily detrimental to life."

Even as they talked and peered into the dimness of the cavern's interior, they heard the scurrying of feet, murmurs, and even faint calls of dismay.

But now the Vulcan's words were interrupted by a shrill voice that called, *"Grang!"*

Grang bowed his head and hunched his youthful shoulders.

The voice shrilled, "Grang! You have led the enemy to your people! Prepare to die with them!"

Grang's head came up. "No!" he called. "They are not the enemy. They say they have come to help us!"

"Help us?" the voice shrilled all but hysterically. "They are not even members of our tribe. Prepare to die, youthful traitor!"

Once again the young Grang proved himself no coward. His head high, he said strongly, "As a member of the Wolf clan, I demand to be heard by the Council of Patriarchs and on my totem pledge to abide by their decision."

"What goes on here?" Sulu asked nervously.

"Keep your hand away from your side arm, Mr. Sulu," Kirk said. "All of you, if possible, try to smile. Our young friend seems to be going to bat for us. Don't do anything to hinder him."

"Aye, aye, sir," Chekov breathed unhappily.

A figure approached them. At first, in the dimness, it was a seemingly unbelievable figure. The head was that of a monstrous black bat, wings and all; the body, small and shriveled, was covered with dark fur.

Yeoman Doris Atkins sucked in her breath.

As the creature came nearer, however, it became obvious that it was but a very old man attired in a grotesque headdress made from the skin of a bat, and in some animal skin, apparently unique to this world. His face was wrinkled with age and there was a malevolent aura about him.

"The wizard-doctor," Grang murmured to them under his breath. "He is not truly a Wolf, but of the clan Shaman, which supplies the wizard-doctors and wizard-witches of all the clans of the tribe."

The small figure hobbled nearer. "I am Muel of the Shaman clan and an enemy of all raiders from space. Hence I curse you to death and—"

Grang shouted, "I demand a hearing before the Council of Patriarchs! These people are—these people are my friends!"

Doris Atkins whispered, "Thanks, Grang. It was a nice try."

But Captain Kirk said to the wizard-doctor, "Our God is evidently not your own, Muel, and it would seem unlikely that your curses would affect us. Take us to your council, since we have an important message for them and words of peace."

The shriveled little man glared at him, saying finally, "We shall see, stranger from the skies, if the curses of Shaman will apply to you. But meanwhile the council shall judge." He giggled evilly under his breath and turned.

The scurrying of feet in the background and the murmuring of many voices had fallen off, but now, about the wizard-doctor, a score of tall, hefty spearmen, weapons in hand, materialized. They appeared to be older, larger editions of Grang, and, like him, they wore ferocious-looking war paint. Handsome specimens, they stared emptily at the Earthlings and Vulcan, but said nothing.

The wizard-doctor had spun on his heels, and now, hobbling, he led the way down what was evidently a side corridor leading from the main hall of the cavern.

And as he went, he chuckled.

Sulu murmured, "He reminds me of a third-class villain in a third-class Tri-Di show."

And Chekov muttered back, "Unfortunately this isn't a Tri-Di show, and, frankly, I'm in no hurry to experience any of those curses our wizard-doctor friend was bragging about."

They made a turn here, a turn there, into one corridor and out into another. A turn to the right, a turn to the left.

Kirk said to his first officer, "It occurs to me that Scotty, up in the *Enterprise,* has lost his fix on us. If your tricorder doesn't work under this pile of radioactive rock, I doubt if the ship's sensors do, either."

"The same thought occurred to me, Captain," Spock said without emotion. "The situation has most interesting aspects."

"Mr. Spock, I sometimes suspect you will find interesting aspects about your own funeral. By the way, I assume you are memorizing these twistings and turnings."

The Vulcan raised his eyebrows. "But of course, Captain."

Doris Atkins said, "I don't know about Mr. Spock, but I'm lost. I couldn't find my way back if it meant my life."

"Which it probably will," Sulu growled. "I wouldn't think a seeing-eye dog could get back through that maze."

"That will be all," the captain said. "Remember, we are here on a mission of peace, and as captain of a starship, I am legally an ambassador of the United Federation of Planets."

"Yes, but have these people even heard of the Federation?" Sulu muttered.

"Mr. Sulu!"

"Yes, sir."

They emerged eventually into a long cavern hall, which, happily, seemed somewhat lighter than the corridors through which they had passed. Their guard stayed behind as they entered.

The center of the hall was dominated by a great stone table set on six massive stone pillars. To the far side of it were seated seven elderly-looking Neolithians on roughhewn wooden stools.

Messengers must have dashed ahead to warn them of the coming of the strangers, since they seemed fully aware of the situation.

The oldest of all, who sat in the middle, said in a shaky voice, "Grang of the Wolf clan, though not yet a warrior among the warriors, still has reached the age where by tribal custom he can demand a hearing before the Council of Patriarchs. If he is denied his plea, punishment up to the death penalty may be decreed. Speak, Grang. You are charged with revealing our sanctuary to the raiders from the stars."

Captain Kirk said quickly, "We are not raiders. We have come from afar to answer a call for assistance. I suspect from what you say that the assistance is needed against these so-called raiders from space. Was it you who issued the call?"

The patriarch looked at him. "It is not you who are on trial, raider from space, but Grang. Your fate has already been sealed. Your sentence is the silent death which Muel of the Shaman clan will shortly administer. Speak, Grang."

Grang was obviously standing before the highest-ranking authority of his tribal society, but he was not browbeaten. He said in a strong voice, "I do not believe they are the raiders. I counted coup on the one who is known as Captain of the Kirks, but he took no vengeance on me. I believe they tell the truth, and thus I brought them to speak with the Council. Perhaps they can truly help us against our enemies."

Muel cackled his disgust of the opinion stated, but the head patriarch looked back at Kirk and his party thoughtfully. "And how did you plan to help us against our enemies?"

Captain Kirk took a deep breath. "As of now, we do not even know who they might be. But we have a powerful ship and weapons beyond any of which you know. As ambassador of the United Federation of Planets I can point out the advantages of your joining this great confederation one day and—"

But the old man was holding up a hand to silence him.

"Do not think us ignorant of Earth, the planet of our origin, Captain of the Kirks. Our bards still sing the sagas of Earth and how our people first fled from there to this planet."

"Fled?" Doris Atkins blurted out.

The old man looked at her. "To flee the large cities that clogged the atmosphere with fumes. To escape the machines that transported men at hundreds, then thousands of miles an hour, and finally at speeds unbelievable. The gods meant men to walk, or at most to ride upon four-legged beasts. The gods designed men to eat the food of the fields or the flesh of animals, fresh from the hunters—not to partake of food from tins or frozen foods. Man is not a machine; he should not live among machines."

He looked away, as though into a far distance. "The bards sing us the sagas of how life was on Earth among devices enabling man to see or talk or hear a thousand miles and more, devices enabling him to kill his fellowmen by the million. Man combating his fellowman in honorable person-to-person combat for sufficient reason is one thing, but slaying the old and women and children, all with a tremendous explosion—this is blasphemy against the gods."

Kirk said, with possibly a slight element of apology in his voice, "Many mistakes are made on man's path of progress, but progress he must. That species that slows down and stops eventually dies."

The old patriarch was nodding. "Perhaps you are right, but here on Neolithia, our people came to find the old way, the simple way, as nature intended it. And here we had found reasonable happiness until the coming of the raiders. Assuming your story is true, that you have come to help us, we refuse your help. We wish only to be left alone."

Spock injected a question. "And all this planet is the same? No industry, modern production, science, schools?"

The head patriarch frowned. "Nowhere. The ancestors of all of us on Neolithia came in the original ship which transported them and then returned, and all are equally against what you call modern life."

"Most interesting," Spock murmured.

The patriarch took a breath, and there seemed to be

a trace of reluctance in his voice as he said, "We have fled to this retreat, but now, through the traitor Grang, you have discovered it. We cannot allow you to leave, perhaps to betray us. Hence we must sentence you to the silent death. Muel!"

Kirk snapped, "Chekov, Sulu, Spock. Alert!"

Of a sudden the huge hall was filled with bowmen—scores, hundreds of Neolithian bowmen—arrows to the string and pulled back to the ear, ready for release. The odds were simply out of the question. The bowmen lined the walls, stood shoulder to shoulder upon ledges and in niches.

The *Enterprise* group had, apparently, only seconds to live.

Captain Kirk's eyes darted about, seeking escape, but there was nowhere to go. The entry through which they had come was blocked by the primitive, bow-armed warriors, and behind them, as far as the eyes could make out, were more warriors.

Kirk let out in desperation, "Comments, anyone?"

Sulu managed a hollow, bitter laugh.

Grang had closed his eyes, his youthful face pale beneath his war paint.

Spock said, a slight element of surprise in his voice, "Comments upon what, Captain?"

Kirk looked at him. "We are under sentence of

death, Mr. Spock. I expect that momentarily the order will be given for these bowmen to transfix us. Frankly, I can see no escape."

Mr. Spock's eyebrows rose. "What bowmen, Captain Kirk?"

4.
ON TO
MYTHRA

CAPTAIN JAMES KIRK stared, bug-eyed, at his first officer. Then he swept his despairing eyes around at the horde of bowmen.

"Why—why, all these archers! They're about to shoot."

"Most interesting," Spock said. And then, as though in sudden comprehension, he added, "No wonder it is called the silent death."

The Vulcan turned his eyes to the malevolent Muel.

"I should apologize. I underestimated your abilities. But you see, your mind is that of an Earthling, as are those of all my companions. However, my father was a Vulcan, and my mental makeup has variations on your own."

Muel's eyes suddenly widened, and he opened his mouth to shout.

The reflexes of the Vulcan, however, were far faster than those of the aged wizard-doctor. His phaser came up and beamed, and the other crumpled to the floor, stunned.

The bowmen were gone!

The Earthlings, and Grang as well, were flabbergasted.

Spock said easily, "A most fascinating demonstration of ESP, Captain. Mass hypnotism carried to an extreme I have never been fortunate enough to witness before. I have no doubt that Muel could have literally killed you by making you *think* you were being shot by his phantom bowmen."

"Fortunate enough?" Chekov blurted. "That's one way of putting it, but personally, if I never witness such a display of ESP again, it'll be too soon."

Kirk snapped, "The Council! What happened to them?"

And all realized that in the excitement of the past

moments, the tribal elders had drifted away into some unknown recess, leaving the execution to their wizard-doctor.

Grang said excitedly, "This way! Quickly! The warriors will soon be upon us."

Kirk looked at him. "I assume you mean the real tribal warriors. Very well, Grang, we're in your hands. We have nowhere else to go. Lead the way!"

Grang immediately dashed off into a small corridor that the others had not noticed before. The group from the *Enterprise* were hard put to keep up with him.

If they had been confused before by the curvings and turnings of the corridors, it was as nothing compared to the path along which the young Neolithian took them now. Indeed, at times it was necessary to drop to hands and knees and crawl behind him. Were there sounds of pursuit from behind? At times they thought so, and Chekov and Sulu, still bringing up the rear, held their phasers at the ready.

However, they emerged at long last on a ledge overlooking the valley through which they had proceeded on the way to the cavern which sheltered the Wolf clan.

Grang pointed to a narrow path and said, "We can go down that way."

Kirk shook his head. "Hold it, boy." He brought

his communicator from his tunic and flicked up the antenna grid.

"Kirk to *Enterprise*."

"Scott here," the Scotsman's burr came through, a trace of excitement evident. "We lost our fix on you, Captain."

"I know. Have the transporter officer prepare to beam us up."

"Aye, sir. I'll connect you with the transporter room."

Grang, frowning worriedly, said, "Captain of the Kirks, we must hurry. The warriors will soon be after us."

Kirk turned to him and said slowly, "Grang, our many thanks to you. But now we must leave. Evidently Neolithia was not the source of the call for assistance to which we are responding."

Grang looked at him blankly.

James Kirk said doggedly, "You must make your peace with your people. You are only a youngster, and undoubtedly when we are gone they will forgive you."

"Captain!" Sulu blurted. "You don't mean you're going to leave him here!"

Kirk looked at him coldly. "Can you think of an alternative?"

"We can take him with us to the *Enterprise!*"

"Today I seem continually to be forced to remind my

junior officers of General Order Number One. In this case, to the section dealing with the fact that a native of a backward planet cannot be taken from his natural environment and exposed to a more sophisticated one."

"But—"

"That will be all, Mr. Sulu." However, there was a wan aspect to the face of James Kirk when he turned back to the young native. "Our thanks again, Grang, and best wishes. And now, farewell."

He brought his communicator to his mouth, and while the others of the group crowded around young Grang to press his hand and say their farewells, Kirk, unseen, closed his eyes as if to shut out a painful moment as he said into the instrument, "Transport room? Captain Kirk here. Beam us back to the ship."

Captain Kirk emerged wearily from the turbo-lift elevator into the confines of the bridge of the *Enterprise*. Senior Engineering Officer Scott came erect from the command chair.

Without speaking to the engineer, Kirk sank into the chair and said to the navigator, "Mister, set a course for the next planet. What was its name—Mythra?"

"Aye, aye, sir."

Scott said, "Then this wasn't the planet?"

"Evidently not," Kirk said in disgust. "Far from

having the equipment to send a subspace distress call, they couldn't have sent even a semaphore message."

The navigator said, "Sir, the course is one-eighteen, mark ten."

"Thank you." Kirk turned to the helmsman. "Mr. Akrumba, one-eighteen, mark ten, warp factor two."

Dr. McCoy entered, his face agitated. "Just a minute, Jim."

"Yes, Bones?"

"See here, Jim, I've been scanning the planet below. It's a primitive garden. There are lakes, streams, beaches, meadows."

"There most certainly are, Bones. It's practically an untouched wilderness, a Garden of Eden."

"Then I suggest that we make it an emergency leave center. Beam down the crew, say one third of them at a time, and allow them to let off a bit of steam. Swimming, fishing, perhaps a little hunting— whatever they can find to do to unwind, relax. The air is wonderful, the climate—"

Kirk said wearily, "I said *practically* untouched. Evidently things have happened so quickly, and possibly you were so tied up in your own duties, that you weren't following our experiences below. It so happens, Bones, that Neolithia has been colonized by what I suppose in the old days they called Nature

Boys. They've deliberately gone back to primitivism. Above all, they don't like strangers from the skies; we escaped from them by the skin of our teeth. I can't submit the crew to the danger of attack, Bones."

"Very well, Jim, but you'll notice in my reports that I now have six crewmen in the sick bay being treated for minor attacks of cafard. I assume we can expect a major attack shortly if you insist on keeping this starship in space indefinitely."

"Thank you, Bones," the captain said. He shook his head wearily. His shoulders seemed to slump.

The chief engineer looked at him. "Something on your mind, Captain?" He grunted. "That is, something a wee bit more than usual?"

Captain Kirk shook his head in self-deprecation. "Yes, Scotty, old boy. I sometimes think that Starfleet Command should allow a captain more elasticity in obeying such rulings as General Order Number One."

Helmsman Sulu entered and, glancing up at the chronometer-calendar on the bulkhead, approached the helmsman's chair before the bridge viewing screen and said formally, "Relieving the helm."

Lieutenant Akrumba said, "Helm relieved. Course one-eighteen, mark ten, warp factor two."

Sulu repeated, "Course one-eighteen, mark ten, warp factor two."

Akrumba stood, relinquishing the helmsman's chair, and stretched hugely. He grinned at his relief and said, "Well, Sulu, did you find any more exotic animals to add to your collection while you were down there on Neolithia?"

"Not exactly."

Lieutenant Uhura looked over from her position as communications officer and chuckled. "What does that mean? Do we have a new exotic animal from Neolithia or not?"

Sulu squirmed slightly in his chair, his face unhappy.

Spock entered at that moment and approached Captain Kirk's command chair. Jim Kirk looked up.

"Something, Mr. Spock?"

"Yes, Captain. I have a stowaway to report."

"A *stowaway!*"

Sulu cleared his throat.

Captain Kirk glared at him. "You know something about this, Mr. Sulu?"

"Well, not exactly, sir."

James Kirk said ominously, "You seem to be unusually evasive today, mister. What did you mean earlier when you said you didn't *exactly* bring a new exotic animal aboard?"

Sulu said earnestly, "He's not an animal and I

77

didn't bring him aboard, sir. I was as surprised as the next man."

"And just who was the next man?"

"I suppose you would say Ensign Chekov, sir."

James Kirk's eyes went back to Spock. "The more talk that goes on here, the less I seem to learn. Where did you find this stowaway?"

Spock said, "In the specimen container we took down to the surface of Neolithia, Captain. As you'll recall, we abandoned it in the clearing. Later, after we returned to the ship, I had the transport officer retrieve it, and I assigned Mr. Sulu and Mr. Chekov to return it to its original storage compartment."

"I see." The captain's eyes went back to the chief helmsman. "Well, Mr. Sulu?"

"Yes, sir. We obeyed orders."

"I see. And did you open it?"

"No, sir. Not for the time being."

"I see. When you two were carrying the specimen container to its storage compartment, didn't it seem a bit heavy?"

"Well, yes, sir. Now that you mention it, it did. In fact, just fifteen minutes or so ago I discussed it with Mr. Chekov. But by that time we were under way, and I was due on watch."

"And . . . ?"

"Well, he said he'd investigate and report to Mr. Spock."

"Mr. Sulu, *who* is the stowaway?"

Sulu cleared his throat again. "Well, it would seem to be Grang, sir."

"I don't know why I bothered to ask," the captain said bitterly. "Mr. Navigator, reverse your course."

"Aye, aye, sir."

From the background, where he had been standing, Dr. McCoy protested, "You mean we're going to prolong this confounded mission by returning to a planet we've already found was not the one we're looking for?"

Kirk ignored him.

Spock said thoughtfully, "Captain, it occurs to me that if we postpone the return of our young savage until we have solved the problem of the distress call and the raiders, he will be safe from recrimination on the part of his people. In fact, he would undoubtedly be a bit of a hero—a worthy return for his efforts in our behalf."

The doctor spoke up again. "If we go running back and forth between these Horatian planets this way, we'll spend the rest of eternity on this—"

"Please, Bones," the captain snapped. He was obviously in a high state of irritation.

He came to a quick decision. "Very well, Mr. Navigator, cancel that order. Mr. Helmsman, proceed on course one-eighteen, mark ten. Mr. Sulu, I am not going to inquire into whether or not you or Mr. Chekov discussed that specimen container with young Grang while we were waiting to be beamed back to the ship. However, in addition to your present duties, you have now acquired one to take care of *all* of your off-duty hours. You are not to allow Grang out of your sight. He will be quartered with you. While you are on watch, Mr. Chekov will accompany the boy. I consider it your responsibility for any violation of General Order Number One."

"Yes, sir," Sulu said brightly.

"And Mr. Sulu. . . ."

"Yes, sir."

"If that young savage does anything—anything at all—to disrupt the workings of this ship, we shall delve further into the odd circumstances under which he managed to sneak himself aboard."

"Aye, aye, sir."

Dr. McCoy said, "I suppose I'd better get the subject of all this conversation into the sick bay for an examination. He's probably alive with bacteria. All we need is for him to have brought aboard some far-out disease native to Neolithia."

In the wardroom Security Officer Masaryk glowered down at the game of solitaire spread before him. "How can you play this game," he complained, "when every deck of cards left on the ship is so worn you can read the backs from memory?"

Lieutenant De Paul leaned back from the scanner upon which he had been reading. "That's the trouble with a good memory. I suspect I've read everything aboard five times over." He indicated the tape before him. "I think I could recite this one."

Uhura, who had been sitting to one side staring unseeingly before her, said, "Why don't you study something? Improve your mind, that sort of thing?"

De Paul grunted. "Can't concentrate. Too sluggish. Did you hear what the recreation officer said? Every class on board has closed down, even those on such subjects as music. Nobody has the push to do anything."

Ensign Freeman looked distastefully about the wardroom. "You know," he said, "I sometimes get the feeling that I've spent my whole life on this confounded ship. And to think I used to believe I liked the Starfleet service."

Masaryk said, "The next time I'm given a questionnaire to fill out, I'm going to put on it, 'Born on Earth, reared on the U.S.S. *Enterprise.*'"

Sulu stuck his head in the door and looked about to check on who was present.

"Sulu!" De Paul called. "I thought you were the only man on board who had something to do in his spare time—training that rat, Mickey. I've been looking forward to a demonstration." He laughed bitterly and said to Freeman, "Imagine getting so bored you look forward to seeing a rat put on a show."

Sulu entered and said, "Folks, let me introduce the latest addition to the *Enterprise,* my protégé, Grang."

Grang followed the chief helmsman into the wardroom. His eyes were wide, but he was hiding his obvious bewilderment surprisingly well. He had evidently been washed and scrubbed clean of war paint in the ship's bay for sanitary reasons, and his fur kilts had been disinfected. He looked, if anything, a bit younger than he had before.

Sulu went through the routine of introducing him, and Grang managed to take it all in his stride.

Here, at least, was something a bit new. All had heard the rumor of the young savage picked up on Neolithia, but thus far none of those present had met him.

"Heavens to Betsy," Freeman exclaimed. "Somebody new. A sight for sore eyes. Welcome aboard, Grang. In the way of hospitality, I'd teach you to play Ping-

Pong if this oaf Sulu hadn't stepped on the last ball a month or more ago."

Lieutenant Chang said, "Showing our guest the ship, Sulu?"

"That's right," Sulu said sourly. "Doc McCoy insists I introduce him to everybody aboard. The doc evidently figures that *anything* new is of some value in keeping us from moping. Frankly, I'd forgotten how big this starship is. Eleven decks thick, mind you."

Grang had been standing silent, his eyes still wide. He frowned at the stringed instrument in Uhura's hands.

She smiled encouragingly at him. "Never seen this particular version of a guitar before, Grang?"

Sulu snorted. "He's never seen any version of a guitar before. His people probably haven't anything more musical than a drum."

"I'll show you." Uhura smiled again at the young Neolithian.

She ran a thumb over the strings, settling down on the arm of a chair. She riffled through a few chords and then began a ballad of yesteryear. The others settled back. Uhura's singing was one of the few items of shipboard life that none had wearied of thus far.

Grang was obviously taken aback. Though he was

83

in his midteens, it was plain that the boy had never
heard modern music before, certainly not of the type
that issued from Uhura's instrument—and from her
throat.

A string went *ping*.

The communications officer's face fell. "Oh, *no*,"
she said.

Ensign Freeman closed his eyes. "I'll bet my left arm
that's the last string of that type, too."

"It is," Uhura said bitterly. She looked down at her
instrument in disgust.

Sulu said to Grang, "Come on; we can't spend all
our time here. I'll take you to the ship's gym next."

"Yes, Sulu," Grang said. He looked at Uhura almost
apologetically. "I am sorry the gods broke the string
on your . . . your box of music."

She grinned back at him a trifle wryly. "So am I,
Grang," she said.

When Sulu and Grang entered the ship's gym, they
found Dr. McCoy there, arguing heatedly with Lieutenant Peterson, the recreation officer.

McCoy was saying, "And I tell you that some way
you've got to spark some competitive feeling. Get teams
organized in some sport or other."

Peterson said impatiently, "And I tell you the whole

84

crew's too lethargic to get excited about anything, let alone sport." He waved a hand around the moderately large compartment. At one end two men were idly handling weights, obviously lacking any enthusiasm, killing time without finding pleasure in the activity.

"Three hundred officers and men off watch, and look how empty the place is. You know what they're doing, most of them? Lying in their bunks, staring up at the overhead, or lounging around in the mess halls. They haven't even got the get-up-and-go to fight or argue among themselves."

"You have got to do your best to stir them into activity!"

"And I keep telling you, I can't drag them in here. To participate in sports, you've got to want to participate."

McCoy cast his eyes upward in despair. "I've already got two of them in stasis."

Peterson stared at him. "In what?"

"In deep sleep. They were showing cafard symptoms. To prevent it from developing, I put the men in deep sleep."

"I thought that was dangerous except for short periods."

"It is," McCoy said desperately, "but not as dangerous as space cafard. And at least it isn't contagious."

They both looked up as two newcomers entered the gym.

Sulu said, "Lieutenant Peterson, Dr. McCoy, have you met the ship's, ah, guest, Grang?"

McCoy, preoccupied, nodded curtly.

Peterson's eyebrows went up. "Well," he said, still scowling over his discussion with the ship's senior surgeon. "I had understood you were younger." He reached out, more or less absently, and felt the other's biceps. "You'll have to work out here in the gym, and we'll see about building you up a—" But his sentence ended there.

Lieutenant Peterson was an average-size man in his late twenties. He was well developed, taught both boxing and wrestling, and was the ship's champion in both sports.

Now, however, he felt himself in midair, tumbling. Luckily he had been standing immediately in front of a wrestling mat. He landed flat on his back on the pad.

"Grang!" Sulu yelped.

The youngster was in a half-crouch, his hands forward in a wrestler's stance. "I am Grang of the Wolves," he snarled, "and no man touches hand to me in violence."

The doctor, who was as popeyed as his shipmates,

suddenly relaxed and barked out a laugh. "Peterson," he chuckled, "you're out of shape."

The other came to his feet, his eyes narrow and his face slightly flushed. "He caught me off guard," he snapped angrily.

Sulu said to Grang, "Nobody on this ship wishes you violence. This officer schools us in sports, in having fun."

Grang came erect, his face burning. "I am shamed," he said. "I do not know your customs. On Neolithia no man touches another in violence."

Peterson said gruffly, "That's all right, son. In fact, that's a pretty good hold you had there. However—"

"I am not your son," Grang said. "We are not even kin, Lieutenant of the Petersons."

In spite of the fact that the Neolithian was just a boy, Peterson was still somewhat miffed, particularly in view of the fact that both Dr. McCoy and Sulu were obviously amused.

He said, "Have it your way. What do you say we try another fall?"

"Another fall?" Grang frowned.

The recreation officer reached out suddenly, grasped the young savage by the right hand, and turned quickly, intending to lever the other over his shoulder in the old wrestling standby, the flying mare hold.

But in a flash Grang had bounded to the side, turned his own back, and swung in a blur of motion in such a manner that the wrestling champion of the Starship *Enterprise* was flung almost to the floor beyond the heavily padded mat. Had he struck the floor, he could well have broken an arm or a leg, since his limbs were outstretched in every direction.

McCoy bleated uncharacteristic laughter. "By heaven!" he roared. "If the crew could only see this. It'd keep them from cafard for a week or more!"

Grang turned to Sulu and lifted one hand as though in supplication. "You told me he wished me no violence," he said.

Peterson was flat on his back again, his eyes closed in disgust, and his mouth twisted wryly—though in good humor. "I give up," he said. "I'm going to apply to the captain to switch me to the steward's department. Grang can have my job."

Sulu was laughing aloud.

Just then the compartment's intercom viewing screen announced, "Mister Sulu to the bridge, please. We are about to go into orbit."

5.
WELCOME—WITH RESERVATIONS

WHEN SULU entered the bridge from the elevator, all was normal. The captain was in his command chair, frowning up at the bridge viewing screen. Spock was at his library-computer station; and Uhura, at her communications station, touched dials and switches. Various other crewmen and officers of the *Enterprise* were at their posts.

Kirk said, "Take the helm, Mr. Sulu. Mr. Chekov has assumed your charge?"

"Yes, sir. Ensign Chekov is continuing to show Grang around the ship."

Sulu relieved the junior helmsman and took his place.

"Standard orbit again, Mr. Sulu. Twenty-thousand-mile perigee. We'll take a look at this Mythra." Captain Kirk reached out to increase the magnification of the viewing screen.

"Spock, what do the sensors tell us?"

"Another Class-M planet, Captain. Almost identical to Neolithia."

"Gravity?"

"All but identical to that of Earth, Captain."

Captain Kirk continued to increase magnification. A city, or at least a town, swam into view. He centered on it.

"Well, at least we have some signs of population and some form of civilization here. What would you say, Mr. Spock?"

"Very interesting, Captain. However, the term 'civilization' is somewhat elastic."

The captain looked at him.

The Vulcan said blandly, "Walled towns, such as Jericho, were found on Earth as early as 9000 B.C., Captain. But I would not exactly call the inhabitants of such Stone Age settlements civilized. By the looks of that city on the screen, I would compare it to a Middle Ages town. We Vulcans hardly consider the period civilized."

Captain Kirk emitted a slight snort and peered back at the screen. "You would seem correct, at that. There are similarities to a medieval walled town. But let us look further."

As they continued to orbit Mythra, the captain periodically increased and decreased magnification of the viewing screen as he scanned the planet. Occasionally new cities were picked up and submitted to closer scrutiny. They all seemed remarkably alike.

"Comments?" Kirk said finally.

Sulu said, "I get the impression they have a world government, Captain."

"Why do you say that, Mr. Sulu?"

"Because every town you've picked up is almost identical. Buildings that look considerably like the temples and palaces from the graphics I've seen of Middle Ages towns of old Earth Europe, complete with what look like fortifications and drawbridges. The rest of the buildings a bit on the drab and run-down side. But each town so like the others that you'd think they were out of the same mold."

Spock was nodding. "I agree. There would seem to be one central directing authority."

The captain mused, "There is that one town, city really, considerably larger than any of the others—possibly the world capital. Mr. Sulu, we will assume orbit over that metropolis."

"Aye, aye, sir."

"Lieutenant Uhura, open hailing frequencies."

"Aye, aye, Captain. Sir. . . ."

"Yes, Lieutenant?"

"They seem to have radio, a somewhat primitive radio, but lack more advanced communications."

"See if you can raise someone, Lieutenant."

"Yes, sir. I'm trying, sir." She continued to spin dials, touch buttons.

Captain Kirk stirred impatiently at the long delay.

Finally Lieutenant Uhura said, "Captain, in the large temple below, there would seem to be a radio station. Not a public broadcasting station, but evidently a communication center. So far as I can detect, there are no viewing screens. They have not advanced, evidently, to television or videophone. Just simple radio."

"Thank you, Lieutenant. Open communication if you can."

Uhura spoke into a mike. After long minutes she said, "Captain, I have someone."

"Put it on my screen, here."

"Aye, aye, sir."

Captain Kirk said into his command chair communication screen, "This is Captain James Kirk, of the United Space Ship *Enterprise,* representing the United Federation of Planets. I wish to speak with someone in authority."

The communicator spoke, and there were elements of both surprise and apprehension in the voice. "This is Pater Delvin, Brother of Communications of the United Temple. How is this that you speak on the sacred airwaves?"

Kirk said dryly, "Your sacred airwaves are radio waves and open to anyone with radio equipment, Pater Delvin. Please put me in communication with your governor or mayor or whatever he may be called locally."

"You mean the Supreme Exarch?" There was an element of shock in the voice now.

"I suppose so," Kirk said impatiently. "Whoever your top authority might be."

Spock said, "You'll recall, Captain, that Mythra was settled by religious dissidents who evidently fled here to escape what they considered persecution. Apparently the government is a theocracy."

"Thank you, Mr. Spock." The captain flicked the control switch, temporarily disconnecting his contact with the Mythran. "Mr. Spock, put your sensors on this. Although our friend below hasn't even television at his command and won't be able to see us, there's no reason why we can't take a look at him."

"Yes, Captain."

"Throw it on the main viewing screen, Mr. Spock."

Spock moved deft, long fingers, and the interior of a room appeared on the screen above. "Most interesting," Spock said.

They were looking into what seemed to be an odd mixture of a monk's cell and an early radio shack. One robed figure was at the moment leaving the room; another sat before a radio transmitter, his eyes wide. He was a heavy man in his middle years, large of paunch, heavy of jowl.

Kirk said to Uhura wryly, "Your opposite number could use a bit of exercise, Lieutenant." He took up a hand mike and said into it, "Who is the Supreme Exarch?"

They could see the monklike figure jerk when the voice came through the receiver.

"Why . . . why the Supreme Exarch is the Extreme Holy of the United Temple."

Sulu said, "They've got a theocracy, all right, all right."

Two new figures hurried into the radio room so far below them. One of the two was a younger man, garbed much as was Pater Delvin, but the other was a tall, vigorous type, dressed in unbelievably rich garments. He bore an air of command as though born to it.

"What nonsense is this?" the newcomer called out sharply to the radio man.

"A call from out of the blue, Your Holy. Perhaps ... perhaps we are in communication with the Ultimate."

"Don't be a fool, Delvin. Here, give me that!" He snatched the mike from his underling and snapped into it, "Warren, Supreme Exarch of Mythra, here."

Kirk said, "Your Holy, this is Captain James Kirk speaking. I am in command of a United Federation of Planets starship now orbiting your world. We have come in response to a subspace distress call received by our Starfleet Command."

On the screen the other, unaware of being observed, let an expression of thoughtful concern come over his face. He considered a moment before answering. Then, "You speak riddles. I know of no Federation, nor of a Starfleet Command."

Kirk said, "It would seem your planet was settled while the Federation was in its infancy—or before. For your information, your fellowmen have spread over a considerable portion of the galaxy. To help in its administration, there are at present seventeen strategically located Starfleet Command Centers. The

Enterprise is but one of the starships continually patrolling the worlds settled by humanity."

The other's face worked in thought. He said, "I fear you are trying to cozen me, for whatever ulterior motives. I suspect you are the space pirates who attack us continually."

"Space pirates!" Kirk blurted out.

"Do not think me childish, you who call yourself Captain Kirk. You are undoubtedly aware of the raids upon our towns and the kidnappings of our churls."

"Churls?" Kirk said questioningly. Thus far, the other's Earth Basic had been excellent.

Spock explained, "An archaic term meaning 'serf,' Captain."

"Thank you, Mr. Spock," Kirk said, turning toward him. "I sometimes suspect you spend your off-hours studying dictionaries and encyclopedias."

"No need to study such works, Captain," Spock said mildly. "A single perusal is usually sufficient."

Kirk turned back to his mike and said, "Far from being the space pirates you mention, we have come to assist you against them, whether or not it was you who sent the distress call. You see, we have just come from your sister planet, Neolithia, which is also beset by these same enemies."

"I know of no planet Neolithia. And understand

97

this, you who call yourself Captain Kirk. Long years ago we of Mythra were transported here in the sacred arks to escape the evils of Earth, as once the Extreme Holy Noah escaped the evils in his ark of antiquity. We want nothing of your so-called Federation, nor of you and your evil vessel, Captain Kirk."

Captain Kirk made a face of irritation. "See here," he said, "as a captain of a starship, I am an ambassador of the Federation and carry appropriate powers. A distress signal in Earth Basic came from this star system. With your permission, I hope to trace it down. As representatives of humanity in its most developed form, we consider ourselves morally committed to assist man, no matter where he has spread. You admit to being raided by space pirates; your sister planet Neolithia has similar problems. We are here to solve them."

The other was obviously agitated and beset by conflicting opinions. Kirk watched his face closely; there was something here he couldn't quite put his finger upon.

Warren, the Supreme Exarch, replied, "And I tell you that we do *not* want your assistance."

Kirk said very evenly, "We have no particular reason to believe it is not your people who are attacking Neolithia and its backward culture. I urgently request permission to land and investigate in the name of the Federation."

"You have no right to make such a request!"

Kirk sighed. "Forgive me, Your Holy. I assure you my orders do not allow me to interfere with your internal affairs or your religion. However, we are most anxious to assure ourselves that the distress call didn't come from Mythra and that you are innocent of the raids on Neolithia. Given such assurance, the *Enterprise* will immediately leave."

A look of quick rage passed over the other's face, but there was thoughtfulness there as well. He was probably considering the potential strength of this starship from afar. "You still request permission to land, in spite of what I have said?"

"Yes. And to be received as fitting an ambassador of the Federation."

"Why . . . why, you have probably not even taken your anodyne!"

For the moment Kirk was nonplussed. "Anodyne?" He shot a glance at Spock.

The Vulcan shrugged. "It might be anything, Captain. In proper usage, a medicine or elixir that relieves pain. For that matter, anything that relieves distress."

"I know the definition," Kirk said impatiently. "But, as you say, it might be anything in this case." He turned back to the mike. "What is anodyne?"

The other was shocked—or did he just pretend to be? Captain Kirk wondered. He had an advantage over the Supreme Exarch. He could see his face, unbeknown to him. Although the voice came through as though unbelieving, the expression didn't match.

"No person on Mythra but takes his anodyne each day! It is a sacred ceremony. It is against our beliefs that anyone upon Mythra not take his anodyne. Why ... why...." The other's eyes narrowed. "You said it was against your Federation's rules to interfere with religious beliefs."

Kirk took a deep breath. "That is true. It is against General Order Number One. However, my crew and I hardly violate your religious beliefs by *our* not taking your anodyne."

The other said stiffly, "That is not how we interpret it. If you desire to land, you must accept the holy communion of anodyne."

Kirk had had enough. He snapped, "Certainly we can discuss that upon my arrival. With your permission, within the hour, I, as ambassador from the Federation, will land with a party of my officers. We will expect to be suitably received."

The other was obviously upset, but snapped in return, "Very well."

Kirk cut off the mike.

Spock said, "A most interesting individual."

Captain Kirk shot an irritated glance at him. "I suspect you would find Lucifer most interesting, Spock."

The Vulcan's eyebrows went up. "Indubitably, Captain Kirk."

Captain James Kirk looked about his small group of officers gathered in the transporter room: Commander Spock, Senior Ship's Surgeon McCoy, Lieutenant Commander Scott, Ensign Chekov. All were in regular uniform, complete to rank designations and even decorations. None bore obvious side arms.

Kirk was saying, "I need not emphasize the delicacy of the situation. The person who seems to be Chief of State of Mythra has taken a rather dim view of our landing."

Montgomery Scott said, "Captain, are you sure my presence is needed? Work in the engineering section is piling up a wee. We've been too long out, without a major overhaul. Even the *Enterprise*'s bonny engines need the sort of work only a star base can provide, from time to time."

Dr. McCoy snorted. "It's not just your engineering section, Scotty. Every department on the ship is falling apart. What's more—"

"That'll be all, Bones," Kirk said wearily. "I'm afraid you'll have to come along, Scotty. We'll be wanting to check out their degree of technology. Do they have space travel? If so, perhaps Mythra, in spite of its cloak of religious sanctity, is the source of the raiders." He looked around at the others. "You're carrying your phasers?"

All nodded. Chekov patted his tunic, as though double-checking.

The captain looked at him. "Mr. Chekov, we'll have none of your trigger-happiness on this mission. We use our phasers only as a very last resort."

"Yes, sir."

The captain looked at the transporter officer. "Very well. Beam us down to that square immediately before the temple or cathedral or whatever it is."

"Aye, aye, sir."

The six officers of the *Enterprise* materialized before a towering temple that architecturally was a strange combination of Roman, Gothic, and perhaps Byzantine. A square, several acres in extent, spread around them. In the background were buildings obviously devoted to governmental and business matters, all of them drab in comparison to the highly ornamented religious building which dominated all. Through the square swarmed hundreds of hurrying citizens going about their business.

Spock said, "Most interesting."

Kirk looked at him. "Something out of the way, Mr. Spock?"

"I had formed the opinion that these people were retarded in their technology. However, here we materialize in a manner one would think magical to them, but they pay us no attention whatsoever."

It was true. The Mythrans noticed the men from space only to the extent that it was necessary to detour about them in order to continue on their way.

Chekov said, "They seem happy enough."

Dr. McCoy growled, "They seem too happy, if you ask me. They're all obviously as pleased as Punch. Given any average large group of people, you'll have some in a state of euphoria, some bored with the monotony of existence, and some will be down in the dumps. But all of these pedestrians are smiling away like Cheshire cats."

It was true. The incurious Mythrans passing by were all on top of the world. The group from the *Enterprise* watched for a time, scowling in puzzlement.

Finally a voice from behind them said coldly, "You are the intruders from space?"

They turned. The speaker was a man in his middle

years, garbed in flowing robes with various ornamentations, from a bejeweled belt to a golden chain about his neck. His fingers were heavy with rings. He made a strange combination of robed religious austerity and ostentatious display of finery. Behind him stood two younger men, both more simply arrayed, their hands tucked into the sleeves of their robes.

Kirk said formally, "I am Captain Kirk of the *Enterprise,* ambassador of the Federation, and these are my officers."

The other said, still coldly, "And I am Pater Stuart." He looked about, puzzled. "Where is your vehicle?"

Kirk smiled. "Back on the *Enterprise.*"

The other obviously didn't understand, but he said, "You have taken your anodyne today?"

"We don't even know what it is," Dr. McCoy said, not bothering to disguise his irritation.

"Then you are not welcome upon Mythra."

Kirk said, "See here, we've already been through all this with the Supreme Exarch. I suggest you take us to confront this Warren, whom you call the Extreme Holy."

"He has sent me to bring you to him," the other said, turning to lead the way in the direction of the looming temple.

Chekov said to Scott from the side of his mouth,

"Did you notice? This character looks perfectly normal—in fact, on the sourpuss side. But the two younger ones both have that silly-happy look on their faces."

Scotty snorted, but obviously accepted the statement.

In speaking to each other they had almost missed the development that had stopped Captain Kirk, Spock, and Dr. McCoy dead in their tracks in shock.

In turning abruptly, Pater Stuart had stepped into the path of one of the hurrying, blankly smiling Mythrans. They collided and the berobed temple monk stepped back and glared. As though rehearsed, his two assistants brought their right hands from their robe sleeves, and, in unison, hand weapons flared.

For the briefest of moments the inadvertent transgressor stood there as though unharmed. Then his figure grew vague, translucent, transparent, and suddenly it was gone. To the very last, the happy expression remained on his face.

Captain Kirk snapped, "Stop!" but it was far too late.

The temple monk looked at him in mild surprise.

"That man! You've killed him!" Kirk snapped.

Pater Stuart said, "He was but a churl."

"But you killed him. At least, your men did!"

"You are mistaken, my son, and would know better had you taken your anodyne today. He has gone to the Ultimate, to exist in everlasting peace and tranquility."

"Why, you cold-blooded murderer!" Scott blurted out.

Captain Kirk's facial expression made it overly clear that he, also, was enraged. However, he said, "That will be all, Mr. Scott." To the temple monk he added, "Lead us immediately to the Supreme Exarch."

Pater Stuart turned again, his own face amused, and resumed the way. His assistants followed, their weapons back in their sleeves again.

"Some religion!" Chekov fumed.

Spock looked at him. "Religion need not be benevolent," he said mildly. "In fact, on the majority of the planets whose history I have delved into, I find that early religion is more apt to be based upon devils than gods. And even when gods evolve, the early ones are inclined to be, ah, a bit devilish. Have you ever heard of the Vulcan god Maripol?"

"No," Chekov muttered, still upset by what he had witnessed.

"As a Vulcan, I am somewhat reluctant to admit that my ancestors once worshipped at his shrine; however, speaking as a student of history, I find him most interesting. When it stormed, or when there were other manifestations of nature such as earthquakes or floods, he could be placated only with the blood of twins. The people, in their terror, sought everywhere for these unfortunates, so that their hearts might be torn out on Maripol's altars.

"No, some terrible things have been done in the name of false gods and false beliefs. You think in terms of the gentle Jesus of Nazareth, but in the far past, especially, gods were not prone to be particularly gentle."

"This isn't the far past," Chekov muttered.

Spock's eyebrows went up and he looked about the square, even as they walked. "On Mythra, perhaps it is," he said.

As they approached the portals of the great temple, the group from the *Enterprise* were still fuming but holding their peace.

They entered an interior of oriental splendor, little resembling an establishment of religion. Indeed, none of those present seemed to be there for the purpose of worship. Those not in robes were dressed in what was obviously servants' livery and wore the expression of bemused happiness as they hurried about their tasks. Of those who wore religious garb, the younger and less ornately dressed also seemed to be of the same happy character.

Dr. McCoy murmured to Kirk, "Jim, I'm beginning to get an idea about this so-called anodyne."

And James Kirk murmured back, "Undoubtedly the

same one I'm getting. But the population of a whole planet?"

"Why not?"

Their gaudily berobed guide led them to the right to a heavily carved door guarded by half a dozen of the brightly smiling young men who were evidently acolytes.

Kirk said softly to his chief engineer, "Any opinion on that weapon we saw used, Scotty?"

Scott whispered back, "Undoubtedly an early form of phaser, Captain. Not as developed as the type we carry, and bulkier, but whoosh, mon, by the looks of what we saw, just as deadly."

"And evidently they have no prejudices about using the things on any provocation whatsoever."

The guards made no effort to hinder their progress. In fact, two hurried to open the door for the small procession. Inside the new chamber—obviously a reception hall—the ostentatious display of wealth was even more pronounced.

Chekov muttered, "Some religion."

They proceeded to another, smaller door, guarded by two of the acolytes, and Pater Stuart turned and said coldly, "You enter the presence of the Extreme Holy, Warren the Supreme Exarch and representative on Mythra of the Ultimate."

There seemed no answer to that.

The door swung open.

If they had been impressed before by the luxurious surroundings of this temple, it was as nothing compared with what now confronted them. They were bedazzled.

He who had faced them—though unknown to himself at the time—on the viewing screen of the *Enterprise* an hour earlier, now sat on what could only be termed a throne. The element of which it was constructed was unknown to the Federation men, but it had a rich, mother-of-pearl quality that was all but breathtaking. Standing around the throne were a score of the richly robed element that the *Enterprise* men were beginning to think of as the senior temple monks, as opposed to the younger, more simply dressed acolytes.

Captain Kirk, slightly in front of the others, came to a halt. The rest of the group stopped before the throne and bowed. Kirk said, "Captain James Kirk, ambassador from the United Federation of Planets."

The Supreme Exarch said, "I have already informed you that you are not welcome upon Mythra, Captain Kirk."

Kirk said, "That does not surprise me, ah, Your Extreme Holy. We have been on your planet's surface less than a quarter of an hour and have already witnessed as cold-blooded a murder as our eyes have ever seen."

The other frowned his puzzlement.

Pater Stuart said unctuously, "It was necessary on the square to send a churl to the Ultimate."

"Oh." The Supreme Exarch shook a bejeweled hand in dismissal of the matter. "A churl."

Dr. McCoy said, "A member of the human race, whose life was just as important to him as yours is to you."

"Indeed?" The religious head looked down at the doctor in amusement. "On Mythra we do not think it so. Did you see the churl's face at the moment of his meeting the Ultimate?"

The doctor scowled.

"Did he not seem *ultimately* happy at the time?"

Dr. McCoy's face worked in irritation, but for the moment he held his peace.

The Supreme Exarch pursued his point. "All men die sooner or later, including you from the Federation. Let us hope that when your time comes you will meet the Ultimate as happily as did the churl, and as happily as do all men here on Mythra." His eyes returned to Captain Kirk.

"Since speaking to you on the sacred airwaves, by

means of which we of the United Temple communicate throughout all Mythra, I have had a change of opinion, Captain. I have decided to accept your assistance against the space pirates."

Kirk said suspiciously, "Ah?"

The Supreme Exarch clapped his hands. "Refreshments for our guests!"

Two liveried servants scurried forward bearing trays, evidently of gold, holding highly ornamented goblets. The Supreme Exarch was served first; then Kirk and the others from the starship took the proffered drinks courteously.

The Supreme Exarch held up his goblet as though in a toast. "To your assistance against the space pirates," he said.

Dr. McCoy snapped, "A moment, please."

The enthroned religious head scowled. "You refuse my hospitality?"

"Not at all," McCoy returned smoothly. "However, I am head of the medical department of the *Enterprise*, and, as such, I must check any food or drink we take on this planet that might affect us negatively."

"You accuse me of attempting to poison you?"

"Not at all, but every planet, no matter how seemingly identical to our own world, has its own local flora and fauna. Consequently what might even be healthful

112

for you, who have spent your whole lives on Mythra, might be dangerous to us."

He unslung his medical tricorder, flicked a switch, and twisted a dial.

Dr. McCoy's eyebrows went up and he said blandly, "It is as I suspected. Is this what you have been calling anodyne?"

"It is!" the other rapped in return. "All must take their anodyne daily on Mythra. Not to do so is to interfere with our religious customs."

Dr. McCoy snorted his opinion of that and turned back to Captain Kirk. "I would have to analyze it further in my laboratory on the ship; however, this drink contains a very effective hallucinogen, related, I suspect, to what was once called *lysergic acid diethylamide,* or LSD-twenty-five, on Earth. Its use in the Federation has long been discontinued, even by medical authorities."

Captain Kirk said to the Supreme Exarch, "Is this the cooperation you referred to? I note, by the way, that although your so-called churls and some of your younger temple monks seem to be under the influence of this hallucinogen, you, yourself, and your senior priests obviously don't take it."

The other's eyes narrowed. "I did not mention cooperation, Captain Kirk. I said that I have decided to accept your assistance. For your information, when our ancestors first arrived here on Mythra they brought few weapons, and, over the years, even many of these have fallen into disuse."

Spock said, "Evidently a good many scientific discoveries have fallen into disuse on this planet. On the face of it, your culture is going backward, rather than advancing. Your priesthood, which abstains from this anodyne, is not great enough to maintain a high level of science, and your drug-bemused churls haven't the intelligence."

The Supreme Exarch's eyes hardened at that, but he shook his head in rejection and turned back to Captain Kirk. "Now we require some of the weapons which you evidently have on your ship, to repulse the space pirates whose raids come ever more often. So I demand that you release such weapons to us."

Kirk shook his head. "I wouldn't do that, even if Federation law allowed me to. Your government is obviously incapable of intelligent use of advanced tools of destruction. We would have no guarantee that you wouldn't use them against your own people or against any future starships that might visit here."

The Supreme Exarch turned his eyes to Ensign Chekov. "My son," he said, "give me whatever weapons you bear on your person."

And Chekov stepped forward and put his phaser in the outstretched hand of the Mythran.

On his face was the happy bemusement of those who had taken anodyne.

6.
RATNAPPED

The other five of the group from the *Enterprise* stared at Chekov in utter disbelief.

McCoy blurted, "He took it. Before I had time to warn you all and before I analyzed the evil stuff, he must have taken a sip."

Captain Kirk darted a look from the Mythran to Ensign Chekov and back again. "And now I suppose you consider that this junior officer of mine is in your power."

The Supreme Exarch was examining the phaser. "Its workings seem simple enough," he mused. "More advanced than our own side arms. Undoubtedly you can supply us with an ample number, along with other weapons." He turned his eyes to Ensign Chekov, who was staring happily at him. "You answer the captain's question, my son. Are you in my power?"

Chekov said blissfully, "All power is in the hands of Your Extreme Holy. Command me; I obey."

The Mythrans who were gathered about the throne chuckled. Their leader, also amused, turned back to Captain Kirk. "And you will feel the same when you have taken your anodyne, Captain."

James Kirk looked at his officers. "Comments, gentlemen?"

Dr. McCoy blurted out, "They'll have their work cut out getting me to take any of that poison."

"Or me," Scotty snapped.

The Supreme Exarch said with deceptive mildness, "I suggest to you, Captain Kirk, that the life of your young officer is in my hands. I have only to request it and he will gladly commit suicide. Does this affect your opinions?"

Captain Kirk opened his mouth to bark a reply, but Spock spoke up.

"Ah, Captain. I suggest that we are in an untenable

position, and hence that you demonstrate to His Extreme Holy the *other* device that you carry."

Kirk stared at him, and for a moment the Vulcan was afraid that his superior had failed to get his message. But then the captain's eyes widened ever so slightly, and he put his hand in his tunic and drew out his communicator.

The Mythrans stared at it suspiciously.

Captain Kirk said, "Its workings are simple." He lifted the antenna grill.

"Cover him," the Supreme Exarch snapped, and a dozen of the primitive phasers that were the side arms of the Mythrans were immediately trained on Kirk and the others.

Captain Kirk made a shrug of deprecation. "By Federation law my hands are largely tied, so far as doing harm to you is concerned. However, if there were any possible way for us to escape, we would."

Warren, ruler of all Mythra, chuckled. "There is none," he said. "Your junior officer is under my domination. And the rest of you are covered by my priests. Tell me what this new device does."

But at that moment the group from the *Enterprise,* including Ensign Chekov, turned misty and disappeared, leaving a collection of gaping pseudopriests behind them.

Back in the transporter room the group materialized on the circular platform from which they had been beamed down to the surface of Mythra less than an hour earlier.

Ensign Chekov, his face still smiling, but a worried strangeness in his eyes, protested, "But I do not want to leave Mythra."

Captain Kirk didn't even bother to look at him, but strode down the steps from the light panel upon which he had materialized and confronted the intercom viewing screen.

He barked into it, "Security Lieutenants Kellum and Masaryk, report to the transporter room immediately, if you please."

The others were following him down into the room. Captain Kirk looked at Dr. McCoy. "Your opinion about the condition of this young fool, Bones?"

The doctor shrugged and looked at the younger man, thinly veiling his disgust. "I'll have to look him over in the sick bay. However, in view of the fact that that phony priesthood evidently makes each citizen take anodyne every day, it obviously wears off in a twenty-four-hour period."

Masaryk and Kellum hurried into the transporter room, mystified.

Kirk said, "You will escort Ensign Chekov to the

sick bay and keep close watch over him until further orders. I said *close* watch. Mr. Chekov is a very sick man, and for the moment I'm afraid that he cannot be trusted."

"But I don't *want* to leave Mythra," Chekov wailed. However, he submitted amiably enough to the two security men and marched obediently from the compartment.

Kirk said to the transporter officer, "A bit of delicate thievery is in order. Down below, in the temple, in the same room from which you just rescued us, is Ensign Chekov's phaser, probably still in the hands of the so-called Supreme Exarch. I would think that with a bit of fine work with tractor beam and transporter you could recover it."

"Aye, aye, sir." The transporter officer turned to his controls, frowning in concentration.

"And, mister, let me congratulate you on your prompt cooperation in that ridiculous situation."

The transporter officer grinned at him. "Your message couldn't have been clearer, Captain. When you said into your communicator that if there were any possible way for you to escape, you would, I just beamed you up."

The captain looked around at the rest. "Let's adjourn to the briefing room and go over this."

A short time later, still disgusted, James Kirk took the end chair at the large table in the briefing room and motioned the others to be seated.

"Gentlemen," he said, "let us have comments on this fouled-up situation."

"Comments?" said Dr. McCoy. "I'll make a comment. This silly mission is a wild-goose chase. I suggest we make our way back to the nearest Starfleet Command Center."

"I might have known better than to ask your opinion, Bones. Your feelings are already on record. What about you, Scotty?"

Montgomery Scott said slowly, "One thing seems fairly obvious, Captain. Mythra was not the source of the distress call, nor is it the base of the beastie raiders of Neolithia."

The captain frowned thoughtfully. "From what you saw, you don't think they have the technology either to send such a call nor to cross space to Neolithia?"

Scott shook his head decisively.

Spock added, "Besides, what technology they have is in the hands of the so-called priests. They would hardly issue a call for help—when they were so anxious to keep from us the manner in which they have dominated their people."

"I think you're correct. The question now becomes

this: What are we to do about Mythra and our friend the Supreme Exarch?"

Scott snapped, "What *can* we do? General Order Number One prevents us from interfering with the internal affairs of that beastie planet and particularly any institutions such as religion."

Spock said thoughtfully, "Whatever the original colonists might have believed in, certainly today the United Temple is made up of a small group of corrupt men who have, through drugs, seized control of the whole planet and enslaved the people."

"Unfortunately," Kirk mused, "we are too far from the nearest star base to get instructions within any reasonable time, even utilizing subspace and space warp communications. However, they would hardly authorize a deliberate military attack upon Mythra's government. We are far, far away from Federation jurisdiction."

Dr. McCoy said slowly, "Perhaps an attack on our part wouldn't be required, Jim."

They all looked at him.

"I'd have to put it on my laboratory computers, of course, but as I recall the hallucinogens, a very minute amount of the drugs is usually required to cause the effect they have upon the brain."

Kirk said, "What's that got to do with it, Bones?"

"Also, a very small amount of antidote would be required to counteract the effect."

"Very interesting indeed," Spock said, "but I fail to see the connection with our problem, Doctor."

But McCoy was continuing to muse. "I wonder just how long it would take for the people of Mythra to revolt against their pseudopriest masters if they were freed of the effects of the anodyne."

Scott said impatiently, "How could you free them from its effects, mon? The confounded religion calls for every citizen on the planet—save the head laddies themselves—to take the stuff daily. They're under its beastie effects twenty-four hours a day."

The doctor was continuing to think his way along, even as he talked. "As I remember, when we first scanned the capital of Mythra on the bridge viewing screen, it was notable that the city's water supply consisted of but one reservoir."

Light was beginning to come through to both Spock and Captain Kirk.

Spock said thoughtfully, "Just how minute a quantity of antidote would be required?"

"As I say, I'll have to put it on the computers. In fact, I'll have to analyze this anodyne drug. Happily, we have poor Chekov all dosed up with it, and I can use him for my analysis."

Kirk came to a quick decision. "Very well, Bones. Go to work on it immediately. Turn out an antidote for the anodyne. We'll manufacture a sufficient quantity to dose the whole reservoir. Your point is obvious. Everybody has to drink water every day. We'll free the capital city of Mythra, at least, from the anodyne before the Supreme Exarch and his gang know what's happened. Then it will be up to the Mythrans themselves to throw off their yoke, first in their capital city, and then, town by town, over the rest of the planet. The senior priesthood is a mere handful. It would seem that freedom, once given a start, would avalanche from town to town."

He stood, preparatory to leaving for the bridge. "If all goes well, we can beam your antidote down to the reservoir at night, and not a soul on Mythra will be the wiser."

Dr. Leonard McCoy looked up from the screen of his medical computer at his head nurse. There was a spark of humor in his eye and jubilation in his voice.

"Why, this is considerably simpler than I had even hoped for. Whoever, among those pseudopriests, first concocted this psychedelic tranquilizer was obviously unacquainted with other than the primitive research in the field."

STAR TREK

Christine Chapel said, "As you know, Dr. McCoy, I have several degrees in research medicine, but I must admit my studies of the hallucinogens have been neglected. The universities in which I worked seemed to have reached the conclusion that they were old hat."

The doctor was still chortling happily, even as he made a few notes. "One fascinating aspect of working on a starship such as the *Enterprise,* nurse. Somewhere in the reaches of the galaxy you will find just about anything—in medicine, or otherwise. On one planet the inhabitants will still be utilizing boomerangs in warfare; on another, aspirin is still used as a cure for headache."

"Aspirin?" She frowned. "It seems to me as though I may have read something about that as a student of medical history."

"A white crystalline derivative of salicylic acid," he said absently. He stared at the notes he had taken. "I think I'll take this down to Scotty. We could probably make it ourselves right here, but I hate to use up so much of our remaining supplies. And he should have most of this in basic chemical stores."

"We *are* running terribly short," she agreed.

Dr. McCoy left the sick bay, still highly pleased with himself, went out into the corridor, and took the first turbo-lift. He requested the senior engineering officer's office and within minutes was in Scotty's presence.

The Scotsman, seated behind his desk, a welter of reports before him, looked up. "Well, Bones, is it important? I'm in a wee bit of a dither here."

McCoy said happily, "Can you do me up about ten pounds of this, Scotty? If you can, we're in the anti-phony-priesthood business."

"Already?" Scotty said. He frowned down at the notes. "Is this all? You mean if we drop only ten pounds of this in that wee loch they have in the hills above their town, the beastie effects of that anodyne will be ended?"

"For at least a week."

Scott threw a switch, then read from the reports into a desk mike.

He came to his feet. "Let's go, mon. We can pick it up on our way to the transporter room."

It was McCoy's turn to be taken aback. "It will be ready so soon?"

The engineer looked at him loftily. "It took the medical department less than an hour to concoct it. Why do you think it should take my chemical engineers more than ten minutes to manufacture it?"

"Pardon me," Dr. McCoy said dryly.

In the transporter room they found the transporter officer to whom the captain had given the job of retrieving Ensign Chekov's phaser. He was chuckling. The phaser in question was sitting on the console.

He said, without need of further explanation, "You should have seen the look on his face."

Dr. McCoy held up his ten-pound package of antidote. "And here is our return present to our friend the Supreme Exarch."

The other frowned, not understanding.

The doctor said, "This is your department, not mine. All we want you to do is transport this down to their reservoir."

Scott said, "Aye, and I think possibly it had better materialize about twenty feet under the surface. Give it plenty of time to dissolve before there is any chance of anybody spotting it. Whoosh, that bunch are going to have the surprise of their lives."

The transporter officer shrugged his lack of comprehension, but took the packet and carried it toward the circular platform and one of its six light panels.

In a matter of minutes the antidote had been transported to the Mythran reservoir. It was all that the crew of the *Enterprise* could do. The Supreme Exarch's subjects would have their chance at freedom.

Sulu entered the wardroom, put his hands on his hips, and looked about accusingly. Only a dozen or so were present, and most of them were obviously burdened with the depressing air of boredom which was now suffusing the whole ship.

Someone called, "Are we on the new course to . . . what's the name of this final planet?"

"Bavarya, wasn't it?" someone else said listlessly.

Sulu nodded. "We're on the new course," he said, still eyeing them suspiciously.

Someone else called, "How's Chekov?"

"He's completely recovered," Sulu replied. "And the Mythran operation came off like a dream. . . . I'd like to know if it was one of you jokers."

Uhura, who had been fiddling with her guitar while scowling at its missing two strings, looked up to say, "What are you talking about, Sulu?"

"Somebody ratnapped Mickey while I was busy with Grang."

Now everyone looked at him as though he had suddenly gone off his rocker.

"Did what?" Lieutenant Chang said.

"Mickey's been stolen."

"Oh, don't be ridiculous," Freeman said, an edge of irritation in his voice. "Who'd steal a rat? Besides, how could anyone hide him? I'll bet you left the door to your quarters open and he got away. Have you had the doc check you for cafard?"

"I'm sure he'll turn up, Sulu," Uhura said. "He's probably running up and down the corridors this very minute looking for something to eat. He'll be happy when he's caught."

Sulu said darkly, "The door to my quarters was closed, and, what's more, I had him in a cage which the boys in the metals workshop did up for me. He couldn't have gotten away on his own."

He sat down abruptly and glared around at them.

However, if facial expression meant anything, all present were innocent of the crime of ratnapping.

Freeman repeated, "But who'd want to steal a rat?"

Lieutenant Chang said, "He'll turn up." She looked over at the communications officer. "Uhura, what kind of a tune can you coax out of that box with only three strings left?"

Uhura looked wry. "Not much, I'm afraid. But how's this?"

She began to strum, then hum, preparing to sing. A string went *ping*.

It was on the following watch that Communications Officer Uhura looked up suddenly.

"Captain!"

"Yes, Lieutenant?" Captain James Kirk had been sitting quietly in his command chair, brooding. An hour earlier he had had another session with Dr. McCoy, who had reported twenty crewmen now in stasis. Kirk was beginning to suspect that the doctor might be correct, that this whole assignment was meaningless. Except for the fact that raiders from space were hitting both Neolithia and Mythra, he would have been tempted to admit defeat and return to the nearest star base for the rest and refitting which he, as well as McCoy, was fully aware the *Enterprise* needed.

Uhura said urgently, "I am picking up a subspace communication, Captain."

"Ah? Bring it in, Lieutenant." He flicked a switch on his command chair.

"Aye, aye, sir."

Captain Kirk said, "Captain James Kirk, United Space Ship *Enterprise* of United Federation of Planets here."

A voice said, "You are entering the territory of the planet Bavarya."

"We are aware of that. Who is speaking, please?"

"This is *Oberst* Muller of Planetary Defense Command. It is forbidden for you to enter Bavaryan jurisdiction without permission."

"Very well," Kirk said dryly. "How do I manage to secure permission?"

There was a short silence.

"Well, *Oberst* . . . ?" Kirk said.

"There is no manner in which you can secure permission to enter Bavaryan space. Military spacecraft are forbidden to enter our jurisdiction."

"I see. However, *Oberst* Muller, the *Enterprise* is not exactly a military craft in the old sense of the word. The *Enterprise* is a patrol starship operating under Starfleet Command of the Federation. We have approached Bavarya in response to a call of distress. I am afraid, *Oberst,* I must request that you check with higher authority and call me back. Captain Kirk, over and out."

He flicked off the switch and looked over at Spock. "Comments?"

Spock said, "At last, Captain, we have come upon a more advanced culture than that which prevails on the other Horatian planets—a culture, it would seem, capable of sending both the distress call and expeditions to Neolithia and Mythra. I would suggest, Captain, that the deflectors be activated. Our *Oberst* Muller might be a bit precipitate."

"Your point is well taken, Mr. Spock. Mr. Sulu, activate the ship's deflector shields and adjust them to the third magnitude."

"Aye, aye, sir."

"And while we're awaiting *Oberst* Muller, we might as well take a look at this Bavarya." He touched controls, brought the planet in question into the bridge viewing screen, and rapidly increased magnification.

"Another Class-M planet, of course, Mr. Spock?"

Spock was busily taking readings from his hooded screen at his library computer station.

"Yes, Captain, remarkably similar to the other two planets, with the exception here that the percentage of carbon dioxide in the atmosphere would indicate a high industrial development and the use of fossil fuels such as petroleum."

Kirk said testily, "I am getting tired of planets that reject our assistance no matter how selflessly it's offered. All three of these Horatian worlds seem to wish to remain hermits among the planets." He increased magnification again and frowned as a moderately large city swam into view.

"Mr. Spock, refresh me on our information on Bavarya."

"Yes, sir. It is the most recently settled—less than a century ago. The original colonists numbered approximately one thousand political malcontents from Earth itself."

"Did you say less than a century?"

Spock looked at him. "Yes, Captain."

"Mr. Spock, as a rough estimate, what would you say the population of that city in the viewing screen might be?"

Spock stared at the screen, and even as he took it in, his face registered uncharacteristic surprise.

"Very interesting, Captain, and your point is well taken. I would estimate at least one hundred thousand citizens. I am assuming that it is what it would appear to be, a city similar to one of the middle twentieth century."

"See what you can find in the library banks, Mr. Spock, that might pertain."

Spock bent over his hood for a few moments. When he looked up again, there was disbelief in his Vulcan face.

"Captain, it would seem that an increase that could be termed a population explosion would result in a doubling of the number of citizens in fifteen years. Even with advanced medicine and the most fruitful of conditions, the most healthful of climates, and the absence of pestilence and war, such an increase in less than fifteen years cannot be expected."

Captain Kirk scowled at his first officer and then let his eyes go back to the city on the screen. He decreased magnification and scanned the planet surface quickly, going over towns, villages, and cities. He finally settled on one of the latter and zeroed in on it as before.

He said, "Mr. Spock, given a doubling of population every fifteen years, which seems a fantastic speed, what would a population beginning with one thousand be in a century?"

Spock put it on the computer. "In a century it would be one hundred and twenty-eight thousand."

"I submit, Mr. Spock, that one city below has a population of at least that."

"It would appear so, Captain."

"And from what we have seen of the rest of the planet surface, it would be difficult to gauge its population at less than five million."

Captain Kirk flicked on his command chair intercom and pressed a button connecting it with the computer banks. He said, "Is it possible for a population of one thousand to increase to over five million within a period of less than a century?"

Within seconds the mechanical-sounding computer voice came through. *"It is impossible."*

Lieutenant Uhura interrupted from her communications control station. "A message from Bavarya, Captain Kirk."

"Very well, Lieutenant, bring it in." He flicked a control and said, "Captain James Kirk of the United

Federation of Planets Starship *Enterprise* here."

A voice they recognized as that of *Oberst* Muller barked abruptly, "His All Highest, Nummer Ein of Bavarya!"

"Another All Highest," Sulu muttered disgustedly.

7.
NUMMER EIN

Lieutenant Uhura, are we close enough to throw this on the viewing screen?" Kirk asked.

"Yes, sir."

"Please do so. I would like to confront, ah, Nummer Ein face-to-face."

Uhura touched controls, and the viewing screen was filled with the figure of a uniformed, stern-faced, military type who was staring directly ahead so defiantly as to seem almost ludicrous. His eyes quickly took in the bridge and a new respect came into them. The bridge of the starship *Enterprise* was obviously the control center of a very sizable craft, by Bavaryan or any other standards.

Captain Kirk said courteously, "I assume by the manner in which the *Oberst* addressed you that you are the Bavaryan Chief of State."

"You are correct, Captain Kirk. And I warn you that we are not so long gone from Earth but that we are familiar with Federation usage. You have no jurisdiction here, Captain, and by Bavaryan law are forbidden to enter orbit about us. Almost a century ago we Bavaryans left Earth and its institutions behind us to find a new way of life. You are not welcome."

Captain Kirk looked at the uniformed strong man for a long, thoughtful moment. He said finally, "Nummer Ein, we have come a long way in response to a distress signal from this star system. Thus far we have been unable to locate its source."

"It did not emanate from here."

"Most interesting," Spock murmured.

The captain said evenly, "That remains to be seen. The other planets of this star system do not have a technology advanced enough to send such a call. When we checked with them, however, we found that both have been suffering raids upon their property and people. Your planet is obviously advanced enough to cross space and, ah, visit your neighbors."

"Such raiders, if, indeed, they exist, do not originate on Bavarya, Captain Kirk. So now I warn you, if you attempt to orbit this planet, we will defend ourselves."

"I suggest to you, Your All Highest, that by interplanetary usage a vessel with peaceful intent is not forbidden to orbit a world at a perigee of twenty thousand miles or more. Jurisdiction of a planet does not extend beyond twenty thousand miles."

Captain James Kirk deliberately turned to his chief helmsman. "Mr. Sulu, if you please, standard orbit, twenty-thousand-mile perigee. Lieutenant Uhura, if you please, a fix on the communication center Nummer Ein is utilizing. Undoubtedly it is located at his capital. We will station ourselves above it."

On the screen the Bavaryan's face grew furious. "I warned you!" he snapped, and suddenly the screen went blank.

"Mr. Sulu, maintain full shields. We shall see what our Bavaryan bullyboys have to offer."

"Aye, aye, sir."

Spock said, "It will be interesting to discover if these colonists have advanced to the point of developing phasers of enough power to affect our defense shield."

Kirk twisted his mouth. "It is to be assumed, Mr. Spock, that the thousand Bavaryan colonists left Earth a century ago with the technology of that period. However, there were but a thousand of them, and I doubt that all were scientists and technicians. Since that time the Federation has had literally millions of scientists at work perfecting such items as the defense shields of starships. Mr. Spock, I suspect we have little to fear."

The ship shuddered very slightly.

"We are under Bavaryan attack, Captain," Sulu said.

"Thank you, Mr. Sulu."

"Shall I lock the ship's phasers on target?" Sulu said.

"Don't bother, Mr. Sulu. Lieutenant Uhura, please open hailing frequencies again and let me know when our Nummer Ein is willing to talk."

"Aye aye, sir."

It took a bit longer than James Kirk had expected. For a full fifteen minutes the *Enterprise* was subjected to the phaser fire of the weapons of a century past. The lighting system did not even dim. The captain nonchalantly touched a switch on his control chair, and the bridge viewing screen changed views so that the officers and crewmen could see the exterior of the

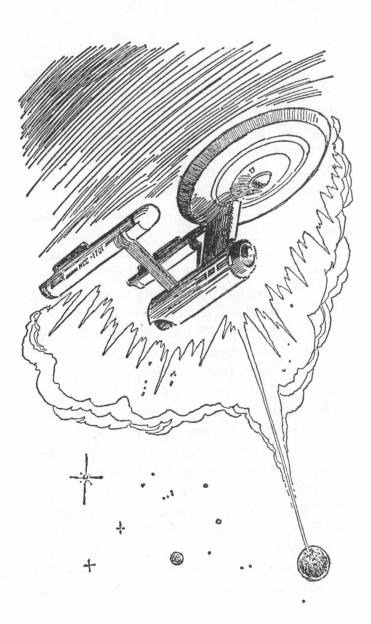

Enterprise. The ship was bathed in an impressively colorful display of pyrotechnics. Beams launched up from the planet below and seemingly splattered themselves against the graceful Federation starship—completely ineffectively.

"Very pretty," Kirk said coolly.

Finally the bridge viewing screen switched back again and a furious Nummer Ein was there.

Captain Kirk said, "I now point out that you, as Chief of State of Bavarya, have taken it upon yourself to make an unprovoked attack upon a Federation starship." He allowed his face to go cold.

Behind the captain, Spock's eyebrows went up, and even Uhura looked surprised at the bluff.

The uniformed Bavaryan blanched. "Capitulation!" he blurted. "Your terms, if you please?"

Kirk held up a hand, as though in surprise. "But it is not a matter of capitulation or terms, Your All Highest. I simply urgently request to be received in a manner befitting an ambassador of the Federation. I sincerely hope that you can give me assurances that the distress call did not emanate from this planet and that Bavarya is not the base of the space raiders. Upon securing such assurance, my ship will leave the vicinity."

"Very well," the other said, evidently regarding the situation as beyond his control. "You and your senior officers are invited to a reception at my palace tonight. We can discuss at that time what proofs you will require."

"Accepted," Kirk said. "Captain Kirk, over and out."

The screen faded, but the captain stared at it for a long, thoughtful moment.

Spock asked, "What sort of proof can we expect, Captain?"

"That's what I was wondering about," Kirk mused. He looked at his chief helmsman. "Mr. Sulu, where is your charge?"

"Grang, sir? Mr. Chekov has him while I'm on watch."

"Lieutenant Uhura, if you please, put a call on the intercom for Mr. Chekov and young Grang to repair here at once."

"Aye, aye, sir."

The captain looked back at Sulu. "How is our young savage doing?"

The helmsman was enthusiastic. "Wonderfully, sir. He's picked up ship life as though born to space."

"Has he picked up such niceties as how to use a knife and fork, Mr. Sulu?"

Sulu looked at him curiously. "Why, yes, sir."

Ensign Chekov entered the bridge, closely followed

by Grang. It was the first time the Neolithian had been in the nerve center of the *Enterprise,* and he looked around in obviously intelligent interest.

The captain hadn't seen the youngster since he had bathed, and Kirk was suitably impressed. He said, "Grang, have you ever seen any of the raiders who have been attacking your planet?"

"Yes, Captain of the Kirks. Three different times. We of the clan Wolf fought them bravely, but they had weapons we didn't know, and they killed and captured many of us."

"You know what they look like? What kind of uniforms they wear, that sort of thing?"

"Why, yes, sir," the boy said questioningly.

The captain turned to Sulu and measured him with his eyes. "He's about your size. Get him a haircut, similar to those of the rest of us. Then get him into one of your uniforms and instruct him to the extent you can in the time available on how to conduct himself as a ship's officer of the *Enterprise.* Ensign Grang, you will accompany our landing party tonight to the palace of His All Highest Nummer Ein."

The group materialized on the parade ground which was the center of the complex of buildings composing the palace of Nummer Ein. A full regiment of armed

144

men, uniformed in gray, was there to meet them, rank upon rank, their faces militarily blank, their bodies straight and motionless.

An officer barked a command, and, moving like robots, the assembly came to the salute.

"Very impressive," Spock said.

Captain Kirk said softly, "Yeoman, I want you to record all developments, both visual and auditory, on your tricorder. Whether or not I will have explanations to make on my handling of this mission when we return to Starfleet Command remains to be seen."

"Aye, aye, sir," Yeoman Janice Rand said. She flicked a switch on the small over-the-shoulder case she carried, activating the electronic recorder-camera-sensor combination.

They remained where they stood for the time. Toward them, marching stiffly, approached a group of what were obviously high-ranking officers.

Kirk asked softly, "Well, Grang, are these the raiders?"

"Yes, Captain of the Kirks."

"Just Captain Kirk," Dr. McCoy said. "It's his rank and his family name, not a first name and clan designation."

"Yes, Doctor of the McCoys," Grang said agreeably.

"You're sure that the raiders of Neolithia wore this

type uniform, carried this type weapon, and looked like these soldiers?" Kirk insisted.

"Yes," Grang said.

Kirk pulled forth his communicator and activated it. "Kirk to the *Enterprise*."

"Lieutenant Uhura here, Captain."

"Keep a close fix on us. Things are already heating up. Have the transporter room stand by."

"Aye, aye, sir."

The group of officers was approaching. Captain Kirk, Spock, Dr. McCoy, Scott, Yeoman Rand, and Grang—now done up in the uniform of an ensign of the Federation spacefleet—turned and faced them.

The Bavaryans halted, clicked heels in unison, bent slightly from the waist, and snapped a brisk salute.

Those of the *Enterprise* were not particularly familiar with this military gesture of yesteryear, but they courteously returned the salute. Grang, from the corner of his eye, watched Scott and duplicated his movements.

One of the Bavaryans stepped forward, saluted again, and introduced himself stiffly. *"Feldherr* Jodl, of His All Highest's personal staff." He half turned and introduced each of the other officers who accompanied him.

Captain Kirk, following protocol, introduced his own party. All saluted again.

Jodl said, still stiffly, "Nummer Ein awaits you in the palace ballroom." He turned and began to march back to the largest of the gloomy buildings which comprised the palace proper.

"Lot of nonsense," Scott said from the corner of his mouth to Dr. McCoy, who was marching beside him. The yeoman and Grang brought up the rear, with Grang appearing somewhat wide-eyed at all the magnificence.

But the doctor was scowling. "You know," he said, "I've seen a lot of troops in my time, but I've never seen such perfect drill in my life. And, do you notice? These Bavaryans have obviously interbred too much. There hasn't been enough mingling of the genes. They all *look* the same."

Scott nodded and scowled, too. "Aye, they do, at that, mon. There seem to be only a dozen or so different types in all. But it doesn't seem to have affected their health. Impressive-looking lads."

They marched the full length of the parade ground and to the massive main entrance to the palace. Here their guard of honor deserted them, save for *Feldherr* Jodl. They entered and came face-to-face with Nummer Ein.

The All Highest of Bavarya stood in more elaborate uniform now, and beside him was a tall, formally

147

gowned young woman. *Feldherr* Jodl spoke introductions, then stepped back and made himself inconspicuous.

Nummer Ein, his face expressionless, said, "We all know the circumstances under which we meet, Captain Kirk, so I will not dwell upon them. We have a reception of the *Herr-Elite* tonight and I shall introduce you to my leading people. And now may I present my daughter, Anna?"

Anna, womanlike, had been inspecting Janice Rand's neat uniform. Now she responded to the bows of the men from the *Enterprise*. She was perhaps in her mid-twenties, blond, and, save for a slight plumpness, attractive.

"Anna," Nummer Ein said, "if you will take the captain's arm and accompany him into the ballroom, I will follow with Commander Spock and the other officers. That way, Captain."

Captain James Kirk offered his arm in the best cavalier tradition and led the way, murmuring, "May I congratulate you on the stunning gown, Miss . . . ah, I can hardly address you as Miss Nummer Ein."

"Anna Shickle, Captain," she answered as they strode toward the sounds of revelry in the adjoining long hall. "And we do not use the term 'Miss' on Bavarya, but *'Fräulein.'*"

"I see. Then your ancestors on Earth were Teutonic in origin, *Fräulein* Shickle?"

"The elite of the Teutonic peoples, Captain," she replied.

Behind them, Nummer Ein and *Feldherr* Jodl were accompanying the remainder of the Federation representatives, and the murmur of their voices in polite conversation could be heard.

Suddenly a whisper from Anna Shickle almost caused Captain Kirk to stop stock still in his tracks.

"At last you have come," she said under her breath, so the others could not hear.

"I beg your pardon?" he said, keeping his own voice low.

"The message. You of the Federation received my message. And you have come."

Kirk closed his eyes for a quick moment of appeal to higher powers. For the moment he could hardly think of what to reply. Finally he said in a low voice, "It was *you*. . . ."

"Yes," she whispered urgently. "Later, somehow, I must talk to you."

"That you shall, *Fräulein;* that you shall," Kirk assured her.

They had entered the large ballroom. All present came to attention and faced the door through which

149

their ultimate leader came, accompanied by the strangers from afar.

Dr. McCoy whispered to Scott, an element of surprise in his voice, "Do you notice? These people don't have the look of sameness about them as did the soldiers."

The Scottish engineer looked about. "Except for the servants. There's kind of a cow look about them, and they look as though they all came from the same mold."

The music had stopped at their entry, but now Nummer Ein made a motion for it to resume.

The Bavaryan Chief of State said to his guests, "Later I shall introduce you to my notables, but now I suggest a glass of wine, and then we'll adjourn to a conference room for our immediate business."

Captain Kirk bowed acceptance to that and raised his eyebrows questioningly to Dr. McCoy as expressionless servants hurried toward them with thin-stemmed glasses upon trays. The slightly effervescent wine was evidently similar to champagne.

Anna selected a glass, presented it to Captain Kirk, and then helped herself to another. The rest were served.

Dr. McCoy had unobtrusively activated his medical tricorder. Now he was the first to hold up his glass and say, "To ultimate understanding between all worlds."

But Nummer Ein overrode him. "To the ultimate destiny of Bavarya!"

Spock's eyebrows went up slightly, but he said, "Whatever that may be," before he sipped.

Dr. McCoy said to the Bavaryan chief by way of polite conversation as they sampled their wine, "I notice a strange difference in facial and physical types between your people present here and the troops and servants. The period you have spent on this planet wouldn't seem long enough for such a wide difference in strains."

For the briefest of moments, it looked as though Nummer Ein was going to snap back an irritated answer, but he controlled himself and said, "These present are the *Herr-Elite*. The servants and the troops, save for some of the higher officers, are but *Doppel-gängers*."

"By which I assume you mean second-class citizens," Kirk said conversationally. "By the little we have seen of your, ah, civilization, I would have thought you beyond the point where there were second-class citizens, a throwback to the days of feudalism and slavery."

"Indeed?" Nummer Ein said coldly. "And now if you have finished your drinks, shall we adjourn to our conference?" He turned to Anna. "My dear, if you will excuse us. . . ." He then led the way to a small room off the hall. The eyes of most of those present followed them.

Nummer Ein took his place at the head of the heavy conference table, with his staff officer, *Feldherr* Jodl, standing slightly behind and to his left. He motioned the Federation representatives to seats, but Kirk shook his head.

"The time for amenities has passed," Kirk said grimly. "The fact is, we have proof that Bavarya is the base of the attacks upon her sister planets. We also know it was from here that the subspace distress call came."

"That is a lie!"

Kirk turned and indicated Grang. "Let me introduce you to Grang of the Wolf clan of Neolithia, who informs us that it is your soldiers that the Neolithians have been trying to protect themselves against."

The Bavaryan dictator reacted as might have been predicted. It took him long moments to compose himself. Finally he said, "Very well, Captain Kirk. I see I shall have to utilize other tactics. Understand this: You are not in Federation territory. Nothing that occurs among the Horatian planets is any affair of yours. The planets Neolithia and Mythra are backward and need the guidance of an advanced culture such as

our own. We are willing to supply this guidance."

Spock said with deceptive mildness, "By killing, kidnapping, and robbing them?"

Nummer Ein flared. "Our expeditions have thus far been but scout affairs, preliminary to landing in force. We are the *Herr-Elite* of the Horatian system, and it is our destiny to help these backward worlds."

"Suppose they don't want help?" McCoy said.

"They don't know what they want! They are too backward!"

"A claim of dictators down through the centuries," Kirk said. "I am afraid it won't wash, Nummer Ein."

"And I am afraid you are in no position to do anything about it," the other snapped.

"We shall see about that," Kirk told him. He brought forth his communicator and lifted the antenna grill. "Captain Kirk to the *Enterprise.*"

"Lieutenant Uhura here, Captain."

"Notify the transporter room to beam us back to the *Enterprise,* Lieutenant."

"But that is impossible, sir."

Captain Kirk stared in disbelief at the small instrument in his hand. "Just what do you mean by that, Lieutenant?"

"The *Enterprise* is under fire intermittently, Captain. The deflector shields are up, and consequently the transporter cannot be used."

"I see," Kirk said hollowly. "I will communicate with you later, Lieutenant. Kirk, over and out."

He turned and looked at Nummer Ein who sat watching him narrowly but with obvious satisfaction. The Bavaryan said, "I am afraid we must reach some compromise, Captain. It is true that your starship has my capital city under its phasers. But I have you— you and your group. What you failed to realize is that we are acquainted with Federation affairs, in spite of the distance. We monitor the subspace waves. We know about your transporters, superphasers, deflectors, and sensors, though until the present we haven't been able to construct such ourselves. Now that will be different. We of the *Herr-Elite* will take over the technology of the *Enterprise.*"

Kirk shook his head. "That is exactly what you won't do."

The Bavaryan dictator said simply, *"Feldherr."*

The officer standing behind him snapped an order, and a score of uniformed *Doppelgängers,* weapons in hand, burst into the room through several doors.

"Search them," *Feldherr* Jodl snapped.

"No immediate resistance," Kirk said to his group.

Each of the *Enterprise* contingent was held by the arms by two of the Bavaryan guards while a third

155

searched him. Phasers, communicators, and tricorders were all taken.

"Take them to cells," Nummer Ein barked. "For the moment we are at a stalemate. I will consider the situation."

"A fine kettle of fish," Dr. McCoy grumbled. "Stalemate is correct. We can't even communicate with the ship. Sulu and the other officers can't bring us back because they've got to keep up the deflector shields and hence can't use the transporter. Nummer Ein is just as frustrated. His phasers aren't powerful enough to harm the ship as long as the screens are up. Ha! What a mess. Above all, we can't afford to stay here for any length of time, since the *Enterprise* is already on the verge of cafard."

The four ship's officers and Grang were in one large cell. Yeoman Janice Rand occupied a smaller one by herself across the prison corridor.

Scott said, "Well, it's up to Nummer Ein to make the next move. There's naught we can do. He'll have to come up with something."

"That's the trouble," Kirk grated. "I'm not sure that he does. So long as he holds us hostages, the hands of those on the ship are tied. And sooner or later they would have to leave, if only for supplies."

At that moment a gray-uniformed Bavaryan officer approached, clicked his heels, and bowed formally. He said, "You will choose three of your number to represent the Federation in the arena."

They stared at him.

"We'll do *what?*" Captain Kirk demanded.

"By orders of the All Highest, three of your number have been challenged under the Code Duello of Bavarya to meet an equal number of Bavaryan champions."

"Code Duello?" Spock murmured. "Most interesting. Imagine a planet as advanced as this having dueling."

McCoy demanded, "What's the meaning of this outrage?"

The officer seemed perfectly willing to discuss it. "You must understand, *Herren* from the Federation, that there has been some discussion in regard to your arrival. Some of the *Herr-Elite* are inclined to take issue with His All Highest about your reception, with the admitted strength of your starship in mind. However, Nummer Ein stands strong. His plan to take over our two sister planets is but the first step in our glorious destiny. He declares that, given access to the weapons of the *Enterprise,* Bavarya can look still farther afield. Ultimately—who knows?—perhaps the Federation will feel our strength."

Scotty snorted, "This half-baked dictator of yours has delusions of grandeur, laddy."

The Bavaryan officer turned to him coolly. "That we will see. Meanwhile His All Highest wishes to emphasize to all Bavarya that you from the Federation are incapable of standing up to Bavaryan manhood—that even the *Doppelgängers* of this world are superior to the elite of the Federation."

"There is no elite class in the Federation," McCoy snapped.

The other bowed mockingly. "That is what Nummer Ein intends to prove in the arena, *Herr Doktor*. And now I shall leave you *Herren* to choose from among your number the three representatives and the weapons you wish to use."

"Weapons!" Kirk exclaimed. "What weapons?"

The Bavaryan smiled his mocking smile again. *"Herr Kapitan* Kirk, it has been found fitting on Bavarya to reestablish some of the old traditions that once applied on Earth. We are a warrior race and enjoy the fray and the spectacle of the fray. Nummer Ein is fully aware of the bread-and-circuses needs of a subjected class such as the *Doppelgängers*. Thus the circus has been revived—somewhat modernized, of course—and is televised on a Bavaryawide basis."

"Get to the point," Kirk said.

"The point is, *Herr Kapitan,* that to make the gladiator meets more interesting, we utilize only the weapons of the days of Caesar. You are given your choice."

"Days of Caesar!" Janice Rand blurted out from across the hall.

The Bavaryan bowed in her direction. "Spears and short swords, *Fräulein*—or any other weapons used in the Roman arena of old." He turned and clicked heels once again. "And now, *Herren,* I will leave you to your selection."

When he was gone, McCoy exclaimed, "These people are mad!"

Spock looked at him. "That is your diagnosis, Doctor?"

"Yes! Dueling in an arena, in this day and age!"

"There have been ambitious dictators before," Spock said thoughtfully. "But it is most interesting that our Nummer Ein even dreams in terms of eventual conquest of the *Federation.* Either he has resources thus far unknown to us, or he is insane indeed. Even if he were to succeed in taking over the *Enterprise,* that is but one starship of the Federation's many."

"If you two will stop discussing Nummer Ein's sanity for the moment," Kirk said, "we'll get around to choosing a team and weapons."

"Well," Scott began, "our lassie Janice is obviously out, and Grang. . . ."

Grang shook his head violently. "No, I am not out. I am Grang of the Wolves, and for years these of Bavarya have raided us with weapons we could not fight against. I demand the right to meet them along with my new friends."

Kirk began to retort in amusement, and then stopped suddenly. "Mr. Spock," he said, "as you recall, did they have wrestling and boxing in the Roman arena?"

"A favorite pair of sports of the Romans, Captain."

Kirk looked at Dr. McCoy. "Bones, what were you laughing about the other day—something about Grang, here, and Lieutenant Peterson?"

Dr. McCoy frowned at him for a moment, but then it came back. "Grang had no trouble proving that wrestling is a highly developed sport on Neolithia, Jim."

"Now, wait a minute," Scott said. "You're not leaving me out of this team."

Kirk shook his head. "Yes," he said. "We can't risk losing you. We'll need the doctor in his capacity. And we need you on the off chance that there might be some manner in which we can use your technical skill to get us out of here. Besides, you two are the oldest."

He looked about at all of them. "The team will

consist of Spock, Grang, and myself. The weapons chosen are the hands. Catch-as-catch-can. No holds barred. Gentlemen, the honor of the Federation"—he looked at Grang—"and the planet Neolithia is at stake."

8.
MYSTERIES
SOLVED

THE THREE combatants from the *Enterprise* had been
equipped with leather gladiators' kilts and with san-
dals suitable for working in the sand of the arena.
They stood now at the far end of an oval enclosure,
which was smaller than the Colosseum of ancient
Rome, but remarkably like that arena of death where
man and beast had died in countless thousands for the
entertainment of the Roman mob.

There were few observers here, however, besides the

technicians operating TV cameras which were spaced every few feet along the wall. This fray was obviously going to be covered from every angle possible; it wasn't every day the managers of the Bavaryan palace arena had opponents from the stars to perform.

There was a small spectators' box halfway down the arena and perhaps fifteen feet above the sand. Large enough to hold only a score of people, it was now being occupied by Nummer Ein, his daughter Anna, and a dozen or so of what were obviously his immediate staff. They were laughing and chattering among themselves as they took their places.

Janice Rand said softly, "I didn't think the girl, Anna, was quite the type who would enjoy this sort of spectacle."

"She isn't," Kirk said. However, he didn't go into what Nummer Ein's daughter had told him at the reception. For all he knew, the Bavaryans had sensors that were delicate enough to be picking up their every word.

Scott grumbled, "I still think it's my job to be in there instead of Grang."

"No," Grang said strongly. "I am Grang of—"

"Aye, I know, lad," Scott growled. "You're Grang of the Wolves."

"Our opponents seem to be with us," Spock said.

Emerging from a metal door at the arena's far end were the uniformed Bavaryan officer who had informed them of the combat, several ring attendants, and three *Doppelgängers* attired in garb identical to that of the *Enterprise* group.

The newcomers made a parade of it, winding up in front of Nummer Ein and his party.

Dr. McCoy said wryly, "Caesar, we who are about to die salute you!"

"Do we have any special strategy, Captain?" Spock asked. In his gladiator kilts his lithe muscles were more than usually accentuated.

Kirk shook his head. "It's man for man. The smallest of them seems to be on the right. He is yours, Grang. I'll stand in the middle. You on the other side, Mr. Spock. If you're successful in finishing off your man, go immediately to the assistance of whichever one of us might need it."

Somewhere, unseen trumpets sounded, and the three *Doppelgängers* turned stolidly and began marching in the direction of the *Enterprise* champions.

"This is it!" Kirk said tersely. "Spread out, Grang, Mr. Spock. Remember, this is a primitive battle, nothing barred. As of this moment you have stopped being gentlemen!"

The Bavaryans came in at a rush, slightly crouching,

arms extended. They were obviously experienced hand-to-hand fighters.

Suddenly Grang, the Neolithian, screamed his tribal war cry and dashed forward to meet his foe. The scream fell off into a doglike barking and Grang was upon him before the slower-moving Bavaryan could recover from his surprise at the noisy attack.

Kirk and Spock stared, momentarily fascinated. Then they had to tear their eyes from this development as they, too, closed with the foe.

James Kirk threw himself into the karate fourteenth kata. As his opponent put up his guard, Kirk rushed him with a left-hand block to the Bavaryan's right arm. Without warning, with his right hand open, palm to the outside, he struck his opponent's face across the left jaw as his hand slipped around the other's neck.

In the background he could hear Grang's voice yell, "Coup!" but he had no time to check on how his associates were doing.

Captain Kirk's opponent was obviously unacquainted with judo, either of the kenpo or the allied karate type. With the back of his hand Kirk forced the burly Bavaryan's head down toward him as he went down briefly on his left knee and then came up fast with an uppercut punch to the other's chin. He jumped back, turned slightly to the side, and lashed out with his foot into the enemy's midsection.

Even as his opponent was falling, James Kirk spun to the right with the intention of hurrying to Grang's assistance.

However, Grang's own enemy was thrown up against the arena wall and was lying in an awkward, grotesque position, and Grang was plowing through the sand in the captain's direction as though he intended to come to Kirk's aid.

The two of them turned in Spock's direction.

The Vulcan hadn't as yet finished off his man, but there was no question of how matters were going.

Larger than Spock the *Doppelgänger* might be, but the Vulcan's reflexes were so much faster that he was making mincemeat out of the slow-moving professional wrestler. Using his hands as choppers, judo fashion, the first officer would step in quickly, slug the other across the neck or face, and step back again before his opponent could retaliate. It was a brutal sight to watch.

Kirk put a hand on Grang's arm. "We're not needed," he said dryly, "and the television audience will get the message the more strongly if we don't intervene."

Grang nodded. "Mister of the Spocks can take care of himself," he agreed.

And even as he spoke, the eyes of the sole remaining *Doppelgänger* foe rolled upward, and he sank, unconscious, to the sand.

As though rehearsed, the three victors turned and faced the box where sat Nummer Ein and his group.

Whatever reaction they had expected from His All Highest, they certainly didn't receive it. Nummer Ein was beaming down at them, almost as though in congratulation.

Even as a group of ring attendants filed onto the sands and began picking up the fallen Bavaryans and hustling them from the arena, Nummer Ein said unctuously, "The end of round one."

Captain Kirk stared up at him. "The end of round *one?*"

"That is correct." Nummer Ein nodded. "When all the members of one team have fallen, one minute of rest is taken, and then the next round resumes."

"One minute of rest?" Kirk said in disgust. "If you think any one of those three men is going to come back into this arena in one minute, you've got a surprise coming."

He turned back to where Dr. McCoy was giving both Grang and Spock a quick once-over. "You seem all right," McCoy said. "That was quick work, Jim. Now what happens?"

What happened came as a shock to the spacemen. The trumpets sounded, as before. Nummer Ein smiled down. "And now we have round two." And the three recently defeated *Doppelgängers* marched back into the ring, seemingly as fit and aggressive as ever.

Kirk, Spock, and young Grang could only stare as the three Bavaryan champions came in at a lumbering run, each heading for the *Enterprise* man who had sent him to the sands but one minute earlier.

There was no time to plan the battle. Captain Kirk fell into the ninth kata position.

His opponent threw a vicious right punch, and Kirk grabbed his wrist with his left hand. It was the same man, all right. For a brief moment the captain had suspected that Nummer Ein was ringing in a new fighter on him; but he was sure it was the same one.

Kirk walked in and grabbed the man's right shoulder with his right hand, slugging him at the same time in the chin with an elbow punch. Simultaneously he moved in quickly with his right foot. Coming around to the Bavaryan's right leg and kicking forward against the man's leg, he toppled him expertly onto the sand.

The other grunted in pain and attempted to roll out, but Kirk didn't release the Bavaryan's wrist. Instead he held him and gave him a heel stamp straight to the solar plexus.

Somewhere in the background he could hear Grang making his doglike war cry, but there was no time to see how the youngster was doing.

Still holding the wristlock, Kirk came down on the fallen *Doppelgänger,* chopping the man's Adam's apple as he struggled to rise.

He came to his feet, breathing deeply. "All right," he panted. "That's the end of round two. Let's see you come out for round three, mister." The other merely looked up at him.

Kirk whirled and headed in the direction of the youthful Neolithian.

This time young Grang wasn't doing so well. In spite of Grang's youthful agility, the Bavaryan had managed to get a strong hold and was slowly bending the boy backward.

Kirk gritted his teeth and muttered, "We have stopped being gentlemen," and came up behind the *Doppelgänger* and kicked him sharply behind the left kneecap. The man screamed and went down and stayed there.

Kirk and Grang, both panting now, turned to hurry in the direction of Spock. However, as before, the Vulcan dominated his opponent with his faster reflexes. It was simply a matter of avoiding the other's bull-like rushes, slowly chopping him down with rights and

lefts to the man's face, and giving judo blows wherever opportunity presented. By the time Captain Kirk
and Grang reached the scene, the Bavaryan had once
again sunk, unconscious, to the sands.

But even Spock was puffing now.

The ring attendants filed in once more, this time with
stretchers, and began gathering up their champions.

Nummer Ein laughed down at them. "Very well
done, *Herren,* but we will see how you fare in round
three. Or perhaps you will last until round four."

Dr. McCoy came hurrying up, his face worried. This
time his charges were not untouched, although they
had suffered no serious injuries.

Janice Rand had acquired water for them somewhere.
She fussed over the boy, who was in worse shape than
either Kirk or Spock.

Grang panted, "Captain ... Captain of the Kirks...."

Kirk looked at him worriedly.

Grang said, "It was ... it was not ... the same ...
man."

Kirk scowled. "Are you sure? Mine was the same."

Grang tried to catch his breath. "He *looked* the
same, Captain of the Kirks, but he was not. He was
perhaps a twin of the first one. But in the first fight
I counted coup on the enemy by striking him across
the face with my hand. It caused a slight cut beneath

the eye. But this man now. . . . He had no cut."

McCoy said, "Perhaps they applied an astringent back in the arena sick bay or wherever they cart those brutes."

But Kirk was scowling. "They didn't have time to give them much in the way of medical treatment," he muttered.

The trumpets sounded, and the three Bavaryans trotted back into the ring and headed for the *Enterprise* team.

The eyes of the group from space bugged.

Kirk blurted, "But I was certain he wouldn't be able to come back!"

"Most interesting," Spock said. He looked at his commander. "I, also, was of the opinion that my foe would be unable to return. But that is he, unless I am mistaken, charging toward us. He has a mole on the side of his nose."

The teams clashed again, but this time the *Enterprise* group moved more slowly. The pace was beginning to tell.

Captain Kirk circled his opponent, who was seemingly as fresh as ever, certainly as fresh as he had been fifteen minutes before, when he had entered the ring the first time.

Nummer Ein shouted down jovially, "You seem to

have lost some of your *élan,* you of the Federation."

Kirk didn't bother to look up. He attempted the fifth kata, but the other avoided the karate position and managed to land a shocking punch to Kirk's right shoulder. Kirk shuffled backward in the sand to collect himself. There was no question in his mind but that his opponent was the Bavaryan he had faced only moments before.

There was no longer time or energy for niceties. Nor could James Kirk take the chance of having the other close with him. The Bavaryan was a bear of a man, and if once the Earthman allowed himself to be taken into the other's grip, he doubted if he had the strength remaining to triumph.

He had to do something quickly and finally.

The opponent attempted another slugging punch, which, had it landed, would have brought the starship's captain to the ground. However, Kirk, moving as quickly as he could, stepped in and executed a kenpo left inside block to the other's punch. Then he moved in quickly with a right forward kick to the opponent's middle. The man grunted in pain, and simultaneously Kirk's right arm shot straight out and he swept the right hand, edge-of-hand style, in a whipping manner to the other's larnyx.

Kirk whirled and shouted up to Nummer Ein as

loudly as he could, considering his breathlessness, "Unless this man has immediate surgery he will die!"

His All Highest seemed to find some amusement in that statement, and various others in his group even laughed.

Kirk had no more time for them or his fallen enemy. He began plowing in the direction of Grang, who was on the ground trying to cover up as his heavier opponent rained blows and kicks upon him. Once again the captain came up behind the Bavaryan and slugged him with a quick rabbit blow across the back of the neck.

When the other had fallen, Kirk helped the Neolithian to his feet. The marks of the strife were obvious on the youngster's face, and he was breathing so deeply that his breath came in gasps. However, he puffed, "Mister of the Spocks," and headed, stumbling, to the assistance of the Vulcan, who was slugging it out, falling back step by step before the onslaught of his seemingly tireless Bavaryan opponent.

It took the combined efforts of all three to bring the single remaining *Doppelgänger* to the sands.

Once again the ring attendants came hurrying out to retrieve the fallen Bavaryans.

Grang sank to the sand, exhausted. Kirk and Spock stood above him, their chests heaving. McCoy, Scott, and Yeoman Rand hurried up, their faces showing dismay.

Nummer Ein called down, his voice still jovial, "You seem to lack stamina. Prepare yourselves for round four."

McCoy, his face suffused with anger, stalked over to the area immediately below the box occupied by His All Highest and called, "Captain Kirk and his companions are in no condition to continue this barbaric nonsense!"

The Bavaryan dictator asked in a mocking tone, "You wish to concede?"

Kirk took a deep breath and managed an emphatic "No!"

Spock shook his head. "Never!"

Even Grang, still sitting on the sand, looked up defiantly and gasped, "Members of the Wolf clan never surrender."

"Very well." Nummer Ein chuckled. "We will grant a slight recess of, say, one hour. At that time the game will proceed, unless, of course, Captain Kirk, you are now willing to communicate with your ship and turn over your library banks to my technicians."

A group of four armed *Doppelgängers* marched from an entry and escorted the *Enterprise* group back in the direction of their cells. The three combatants

175

were so exhausted that the others each gave them an arm in help.

"One hour recess," Kirk ground out from between his teeth. "Hardly a breather."

They preceded their four guards down the corridor in the direction of the cells. The cell doors were open and the five men began to file into the one they had been assigned. Suddenly they stopped.

Anna Shickle, daughter of Nummer Ein, emerged from the cell of Janice Rand. In her right hand was a phaser, one of those taken from the *Enterprise* officers by the *Feldherr's* men. Her face was expressionless as she brought the weapon up.

"Look out!" Scotty yelled, misunderstanding.

Coolly and calmly she leveled the phaser and beamed the four guards down.

The Federation group stood for a moment in shock. Then McCoy gasped, "But you've just killed those four men—your own people."

She looked at him strangely. "They were only *Doppelgängers.*"

Kirk said, appalled in spite of the situation, "Despite your class differences here on Bavarya, those were men you cut down. You murdered them."

She shook her head. "You don't understand. Don't you know the meaning of the word *Doppelgänger?*"

"Doppelgänger," Spock said. "Of course I know the meaning of the word, a Teutonic term signifying 'duplicate,' or 'copy.' But it had not occurred to me. . . ."

Anna said, extending the phaser toward Captain Kirk, "On Bavarya we have two classifications, the *Herr-Elite,* who are real people, and the *Doppelgängers,* who are duplicated over and over again. We chose, long years past, those most suited to be soldiers, then made them over and over. The same with servants and factory or field hands. Actually there are only a few tens of thousands of the *Herr-Elite* on all the planet."

McCoy was aghast. "The technique is not unknown back on the Federation worlds, but it is certainly not utilized on human beings. Certainly our sensors can completely analyze the composition of any human body, but long ago we discovered that in attempting to duplicate the body a prime ingredient is missing—that which is called the psyche, or, if you wish, the soul. That spark of something which differentiates man from the animal."

Kirk said, "These *Doppelgängers* of yours—in short, they're *zombies.*" He had taken the weapon away from her. Now she produced a communicator from her clothing and handed it over, as well.

Spock murmured, "Most interesting. Now I see why

177

our Nummer Ein thinks in terms of ultimately challenging even the Federation. He has at his disposal literally unlimited numbers of soldiers."

Kirk said to the girl, "And you've revolted against this situation. It was you who sent the call for help. Why?"

"Why?" she asked, a sad, somewhat wistful quality in her voice. "Possibly because once I loved my father."

"Your father," Grang growled contemptuously.

She looked at the boy. "My real father. You see, Nummer Ein is not my father. He is a *Doppelgänger* of my father, who I am sure is now dead. I am the only one who knows it among the *Herr-Elite,* but Nummer Ein himself is a soulless copy of a real man. And now, if you will all follow me. . . ."

She led the way down the corridor in the opposite direction from that from which they had just come.

Kirk said, a question in his voice, "And out there in the arena—those three, ah . . . *Doppelgängers* we just fought?"

"You didn't fight three, of course, but nine copies of three men, which is the reason why Nummer Ein was so amused. You see, Captain, he could have sent in ninety, or even nine thousand, for that matter. Perfect duplicates."

They hurried after her.

"Where are you going? What is your plan?" Kirk demanded.

She said over her shoulder, "We are going to the duplicating banks. There is but one set. Long ago our technicians lost the ability to build new ones."

That meant nothing to the men from the *Enterprise,* but they saved their short breath. They soon lost their sense of direction in the maze of halls and corridors. The total area of the palace of Nummer Ein was even greater than they had previously estimated. At long last they came to a bank of early-type elevators and hustled into one. Anna spoke into a tube, and the chamber began to rise.

A robot voice said, "You are entering the Forbidden Rooms. Identify yourselves immediately or you will be destroyed."

This was evidently no problem. Anna held up her hand to a small viewing screen so that the fingerprints could be read. The voice was heard no more. She was, after all, Anna Shickle.

They emerged into a gigantic hall of electronic equipment and long banks of files. "Here you are," she said.

Kirk looked at her, puzzled. "What is your plan?"

She shook her head. "I have none. I was forced into immediate action by your situation, and I had no time.

Nummer Ein planned to have *Doppelgängers* made of all of you and return them to your starship. Your shipmates would never have known the difference, and your replicas would have been in his power."

Kirk frowned at her. "Why? How does your *Herr-Elite* keep the *Doppelgängers* under control? I'd think they'd revolt."

She shook her head. "They dare not. Here in this room are the records for each *Doppelgänger* on Bavarya. Any sign of revolt from one of them, or any group of them, and the *Herr-Elite* technicians simply come up here, take out that individual's record, and destroy him."

"Destroy him how?" Scott asked.

"I don't know, but he simply disappears."

Spock looked up and down the long banks of equipment, some of it recognizable, some not. "Most interesting," he said.

"That's a great contribution," Kirk muttered. His own eyes were darting over the endless machinery. "Scotty, comments?"

The engineer was scowling. His voice, as always when under pressure, had the heavy Scottish burr of his youth. "I don't know," he said. "Mon, it would take me forever to trace out the beastie circuits and figure out the workings of all this."

Kirk darted a look at Anna. "Where is everybody? How long will it be before somebody comes?"

She shook her head. "Only a selected few of the *Herr-Elite* technicians and scientists are allowed in here. They know how to operate and repair the equipment, but they could never rebuild it. Right now they are all undoubtedly at the viewing screens watching the arena show. When it is discovered you have escaped, undoubtedly some will rush here."

Kirk snapped, "Scotty, Spock—get at it. Bones, any comments?"

McCoy's eyes were narrow in thought. "Jim, as I remember, in the experiments that took place in this field long ago, the person duplicated had a matrix— a mold or impression. Wipe clean the matrix and the duplicate simply reverted to the molecules of which it was composed." He made a motion toward the banks of files. "Undoubtedly those contain the matrixes of every *Doppelgänger* on Bavarya. But beyond that, I know nothing."

Kirk drew the communicator Anna had given him from the small pouch in his gladiator kilts and raised the antenna grid. "Captain Kirk to the *Enterprise*."

When Uhura's answer came, there was relief in the communications officer's voice. "Lieutenant Uhura here, Captain. We've been worried about you."

"Is the ship still under fire, Lieutenant?"

"Yes, sir. Not always, but intermittently. We don't dare lower the deflector shields."

"Mr. Sulu, please."

Sulu's voice came through. "Aye, aye, Captain."

"Mr. Sulu, get a fix on us. I want the ship's sensors and computers, the full efforts of the electronic brain of the *Enterprise,* concentrated on this hall. The problem is to determine the workings of the equipment the hall contains. At once, Mr. Sulu. I'll keep in touch."

"Aye, aye, Captain. How much time do we have?"

"None. Over and out."

Kirk turned back to the others. "Scotty?"

Scott and Spock had both been going from one piece of equipment to another, shaking their heads in bafflement. "Time, Captain," Scott said. "If I only had time I could easily figure out every machine in the place."

"We need inspiration now. We don't have time. The most we can expect is one hour from the time we left the arena. Our absence will be discovered then, if not sooner. And we've already used the greater part of it getting here."

Yeoman Janice Rand said in sudden excitement, "Captain! That bank of dials and switches over there. The one with the impressive chair before it."

Kirk looked at her and then where she was pointing. "What of it? There are a score of what are obviously some sort of control panels in this hall."

"But none with a chair that . . . that fancy. It must be the seat of someone particularly important."

Kirk looked at Anna. "Comments?"

She said slowly, "I have been in here only once before. When I was a little girl my father brought me. I . . . I think he sat there."

"Scott!" Kirk snapped. "See what you can find."

The engineer hurried in the direction of the control banks in question. Behind them they could hear the elevator begin to hum.

The whole group hurried over to where Scott was staring down in despair at the electronic control board. "Whoosh, mon, I haven't *time!*" he protested. He stared at dials, switches, buttons, and levers and shook his head.

Kirk activated his communicator. "Kirk to the *Enterprise*. Nothing?"

"Uhura here," the voice came back urgently. "No, sir. We've got the fix on your group, but so far, nothing."

"Put the computer voice directly on."

"Aye, aye, sir."

Scott had plumped himself down in the elaborate chair, his hands racing over the various controls, but he restrained himself from actually attempting to manipulate devices he didn't understand.

"This red switch," he muttered. "There's a wee control lock on it—to prevent it from being accidently activated, undoubtedly. But what's it for? What does it do?" He threw off the lock. "I don't dare move it."

Behind them a voice screamed, "Don't touch anything!"

All spun around.

Nummer Ein stood there, his eyes glaring madness. In his hand was one of the phasers he had appropriated from the captain and his group.

Spock said mildly, "I might point out that the weapon you hold is mine. While it was being taken from me, I shifted its selection lever to overload. I do not recommend that you press the trigger, Nummer Ein."

The robot-like computer voice of the *Enterprise* came through the communicator held in Kirk's hand. *"The red lever will wipe the matrixes of every duplicated human being on the planet Bavarya."*

"Don't touch . . ." Nummer Ein began to shrill, and even as he did he moved his gun hand in a spraying motion and depressed the trigger.

He and that part of the room, including a sizable portion of the wall and elevator banks, blew up in a

184

thunderous explosion. Unbelievably, none of the *Enterprise* contingent was harmed. Gathered around Scott before the control desk, they had been far enough off to be safe.

Spock's eyebrows went up. As he stared at the body of Nummer Ein sprawled on the floor he said, "It would seem that he doubted my word."

Kirk said to his senior engineer, "All right, Scotty. Throw the lever and let's see what we get."

The engineer pushed it forward. Nothing seemed to have happened.

But Janice Rand gasped, "Look!" and pointed. The fallen body of Nummer Ein had disappeared.

Kirk held his communicator to his mouth. "Kirk to the *Enterprise*."

"Yes, Captain. Sulu here."

"Is the ship still under fire?"

"Not at the moment, Captain."

Kirk looked at Anna. "Are the phasers that have been bombarding the ship operated by *Herr-Elite* or *Doppelgängers?*"

"*Doppelgängers,* with the exception of a few *Herr-Elite* higher officers."

"Can the officers operate the equipment without the aid of the men?"

"I . . . I wouldn't think so."

Kirk said into the communicator, "Take a chance, Mr. Sulu. Drop the defensive screens long enough to bring us up. Notify the transporter room."

"Aye, aye, sir."

Kirk turned to Anna Shickle. "We'll leave now. There is nothing more for us to do. I would suggest you destroy this room and its contents with this phaser I'll leave you. Without the room, you and the others of the *Herr-Elite* will have no *Doppelgängers* to do your work and to maintain your military machine. That will mean you will have to buckle down for yourselves to a new way of life. Let us hope that in the future, when Bavaryans reach out into space again toward neighboring planets, they will go in peace and with a real desire to help the others in their march to a higher state of civilization."

Anna nodded. "I have friends, of course. We have an underground organization which was directed against Bavarya's present policies. Not all of the *Herr-Elite* believed in Nummer Ein's teachings." She looked at Grang. "Someday we may meet again, young man from Neolithia. I suspect that when you return you will no longer be satisfied with stone weapons and skins to wear; you will be a spark that starts your people to resume the march of progress."

Grang said stiffly, "I am not sure. We of the Wolves

are a proud clan." However, he looked at Kirk, then Scott, and suddenly grinned. "Nevertheless, I begin to suspect that iron makes a better blade than flint. Perhaps there are a few changes which might be made on Neolithia."

9.
MICKEY
AGAIN

CAPTAIN JAMES KIRK was sprawled in his command chair, staring unseeingly at the bridge viewing screen, when Dr. McCoy approached from the elevator.

Kirk looked up and smiled. "Well, Bones, you should be happy; at long last you have your wish. We're on course to the nearest star base. Mission accomplished, as always when the *Enterprise* is involved."

McCoy said grumpily, "I suggest you have Commander Spock reset your watches, Jim."

Kirk frowned. "How do you mean?"

"I mean that Nurse Christine Chapel and I have forty men and women in stasis, and the number is increasing steadily."

"Forty! In deep sleep? Have you gone completely around the corner, Bones? We won't be able to work the ship."

McCoy said grimly, "Jim, it's the only thing we've been able to hit upon, and we're going to that extreme only with the more severe cases. Half this ship's complement is showing the preliminary symptoms of space cafard. How long it will be before Nurse Chapel or I makes a mistake and underdiagnoses a serious case is in the laps of the gods. One cafard-crazed crewman running berserk through the ship and the mental contagion will spread like a forest fire, Jim. The whole ship could fall apart within the hour."

Kirk, as well as every other person on the bridge, was staring in dismay at the ship's doctor.

Kirk said, "What are the symptoms? How can you tell if a man's about to go over the edge, Bones?"

McCoy looked him straight in the face. He said very slowly, "That tic in your left eye, Jim. You've been under too much strain for too long. I suggest you come to the sick bay for a checkup after your watch is over. Rank has no privileges so far as cafard is concerned."

James Kirk slumped slightly in his command chair as though very tired. He shook his head wearily, as if attempting to reject what the other had just said.

A messman from the steward department came around with coffee. Kirk wanted none, but McCoy took a cup and sipped at it.

He said, "How did the landing of young Grang come off?"

Captain Kirk stirred and said, "Fine. We launched one of the shuttlecraft and hovered above the entrance of the Wolf clan cave. Then, using the loudspeaker, we gave them the full story, puffing up Grang to the skies and letting it be known that through his efforts the raiders will never again be seen. They welcomed him as though he were a Greek hero straight out of Homer."

Ensign Chekov entered from the elevator and was unable to repress his chuckling.

Kirk looked over at him. "Someone has managed to find something humorous on the *Enterprise* these days, Mr. Chekov?" There was a seldom heard tone of irritation in the voice of Captain James Kirk.

The younger officer wasn't put off, however. He said, "Yes, sir. It was Mickey, sir."

"Mickey!" Sulu blurted out from his helmsman's chair nearby.

Lieutenant Uhura said, "The rat? See, Sulu, I told you he'd turn up again."

Ensign Chekov was explaining to the captain. "Taylor and I saw him running down a corridor, sir. It was very funny. He wasn't exactly running—he was kind of dancing along. We almost caught him for Sulu, but he got away."

Dr. McCoy's cup clattered and his coffee spilled over, unnoticed. "Dancing!" he snapped.

Chekov looked at him in surprise. "Sure, Doc. He danced along. Sometimes he even kind of got up on his hind legs."

Dr. McCoy darted for the elevator.

Kirk, astonished, called, "Where are you off to, Bones?"

"The sick bay!" the other called over his shoulder and was gone.

Kirk grunted. "All this obsession with space cafard. I'm beginning to suspect Bones has a case of it himself."

Sulu's face was white.

Kirk noticed the stricken expression. "What's the matter with you, Mr. Sulu? Has everybody on this bridge suddenly gone around the bend?"

Sulu blurted, *"Plague!"*

"What are you talking about?" Kirk demanded.

"Sir, back when Mr. Spock first told me that Mickey

wasn't an exotic alien life form, but merely a rat originally from Earth, I looked the subject up in the library. I read all about rats, sir. Back in the old days on Earth rats carried bubonic plague. When they have it themselves, they act queer. Sometimes they seem to dance."

Kirk snapped, "Lieutenant, give me the sick bay on the intercom at once."

"Aye, aye, sir."

The sick bay faded in. Dr. McCoy was bent over a computer hood, Nurse Christine Chapel immediately behind him. There was a feeling of tension in the air.

Kirk barked, "Well?"

McCoy looked up into the screen and ran his tongue over his underlip. "Bubonic plague," he said. "Also known as the black death, from the dark-colored spots of blood under the skin which accompany it. In the past the disease caused the deaths of millions, particularly during the Middle Ages when it is estimated that three-quarters of the population of Europe was wiped out in one epidemic. It was caused by the *Bacillus pestis,* which is transmitted by the rat flea. Its symptoms include vomiting, diarrhea, hemorrhaging, swelling of the joints, and discoloration of the skin. The disease lasts from one to thirty days and is usually fatal. It has been completely unknown in the Federation planets, having disappeared from Earth in the late twentieth century. The vaccine was always effective, according to my records here."

Kirk said, "What does it all boil down to, so far as the *Enterprise* is concerned, Bones?"

McCoy's face was wan. "If that elusive rat is carrying bubonic plague, Captain, I. . . ."

"What if he is? We'll just have to give the whole crew shots for—"

But McCoy was shaking his head. "Captain, there hasn't been a case of plague on Earth or any of the Federation planets for centuries. I haven't any vaccine."

There was a long, pregnant silence. Not an officer or crewman on the ship's bridge made a sound.

Finally Kirk said softly, "What will we have to do, Dr. McCoy?"

"We've got to destroy that animal. How much longer is the cruise to last, Captain?"

"Possibly three months, now that we're finally on our way back."

Dr. McCoy took a deep breath and said, "If any of us ever expect to see our homes again, we must find Mickey. We may all be dead before the *Enterprise* ever gets back to the Federation, but even if we aren't we'll never see our homes again until that rat is eliminated."

Kirk scowled. "What do you mean by that?"

"I mean there hasn't been any bubonic plague on any Federation planet for centuries, and most certainly nobody from the *Enterprise* would be allowed to land until the ship was pronounced free of danger from it. We'd be quarantined, Captain."

"Holy smokes!" Chekov blurted. "This gets serious!"

Captain Kirk's eyes went to Sulu. "Mr. Sulu, undoubtedly you know more about this . . . this Mickey, as you named him, than anyone else. The responsibility is yours. Requisition any men or equipment you need. Your orders are to *get that rat!*"

Sulu came to his feet. "Aye, aye, sir."

Spock said, "Just a minute, Captain."

"Well, Mr. Spock? Comments?"

"Captain, a short time ago Dr. McCoy announced that he now had forty of the ship's personnel in stasis as a precaution against cafard. The *Enterprise* is understaffed, particularly in Mr. Scott's engine section, where they're working on a round-the-clock basis trying to keep the ship's engines in shape to provide us with as high a warp factor as possible."

"Your point, Mr. Spock?"

"I don't see where Mr. Sulu is going to find the manpower for his search."

McCoy spoke up in the intercom screen. "Cafard is

based on monotony and boredom carried to the ultimate extreme. I don't think men searching the ship with their lives at stake would be subject to boredom. I'll release my patients from stasis."

Kirk said, "Very good, Doctor. But just one other thing. Can't you devise a new vaccine, or whatever, in the sick bay laboratory to handle this potential plague epidemic?"

McCoy looked at him testily. "I can try, Jim. However, I might point out that I have been warning you for many months that the supplies of the *Enterprise* are depleted far beyond the point that makes sense. Not just engine room supplies and steward department supplies, but medical supplies as well. But there's another problem."

"Yes?"

"Jim, in the ship's library computer banks would you expect to find under the heading of engineering, or whatever, a description of a wheel and how to build it?"

Kirk didn't follow him. "A wheel?"

"Yes. A common wheel. Man has been making wheels since shortly after he emerged from the caves. It's been a problem we solved thousands of years ago."

"I don't get the connection, Bones."

McCoy said impatiently, "Captain, the problem of

196

bubonic plague was solved centuries ago. Nobody's interested in it anymore except historians, perhaps. To make it short, Jim, there is no information in my medical computer banks dealing with bubonic plague." His face faded from the screen.

Kirk turned worriedly to his first officer. "Mr. Spock, if you please, check the ship's central library computer banks for any and all information on the Middle Ages disease, the bubonic plague. You might also cross-check under the black death."

"Yes, Captain." Spock bent over his hooded screen.

Kirk touched a button on his command chair. "All hands. This is the captain. Now hear this. The ship is in a condition of emergency alert. A small animal brought aboard as a pet has been lost somewhere on the ship. It is now reported that it is most likely carrying a virulent disease, once known as plague. Dr. McCoy has revealed that even if we can avoid an epidemic which would decimate the ship's complement, we would be placed in quarantine upon arrival at the nearest star base. If the *Enterprise* is successfully to complete this mission, the rat, Mickey, must be found and destroyed."

With the assistance of all hands, Sulu went about Operation Mickey with an efficient thoroughness. The briefing room was set up as command headquarters of the search. To the extent possible, the search teams were assigned to the areas of the ship they knew best. Engine men combed the engineering section; "deck" men searched the main saucer section of the vessel; the storage compartments, galleys, and mess halls were given a thorough going-over by members of the steward department.

All crew members were issued clothing which could be tied tightly about the cuffs and even at the collar— protection, it was hoped, against the rat flea and its deadly bacillus.

Every square inch was explored. Sulu's men progressed from one compartment to the next, searching each room with a care that would have made impossible the hiding of a cockroach. After each compartment was searched, its spacetight doors were locked, nor were they allowed open again until there were several other safe compartments between it and the balance of the unsearched ship.

Operation Mickey went on ruthlessly, carefully. It began in the nose of the ship, covered the bridge, and combed back toward the stern and then down into the engineering section.

The work had the full cooperation and sympathy of the entire ship's company. Gambling was taboo in

198

space, but it was known that there was a pool among the crew on just when Mickey would bite the dust. One of the ship's clerks even instituted a bulletin, which was broadcast over the intercom every half hour, on the progress of the search. Interest peaked.

In the wardroom Lieutenant Uhura, down now to two strings on her guitar, began the composition of "The Saga of Mickey the Space Rat." She left the last stanza incomplete, explaining that it was reserved for the final fate of Mickey.

Finally Sulu emerged onto the bridge, attired in the uniform of the search, cuffs tied tight, phaser pistol at his belt. He approached the captain's command chair and came to attention.

"Eh?" Kirk said. "Got him at last, huh? Where was he, Mr. Sulu? I imagine down in one of the food storage holds."

Sulu moistened his lips. "Sir, we searched every compartment in this ship."

"I know you did, Mr. Sulu. It was a fantastic job in its thoroughness. It's unnecessary to go into details. Where was the little beast?"

"We didn't find him, sir."

Captain James Kirk shot to his feet. "What!"

Sulu said desperately, "Captain, I have one last plan that simply can't fail."

Kirk stared at him. "What do you mean?"

"Well, sir, it might seem a little unorthodox, but Mickey couldn't possibly escape."

"Very well, Mr. Sulu. But this seems to be taking a ridiculously long time. Get on with it."

Sulu hesitated. Then, taking a deep breath, he said, "Sir, my plan is to saturate the ship with chlorine gas."

"Chlorine gas!"

"Yes, sir," Sulu said. "The whole ship. Every compartment, every room, every nook and corner, every cranny, with chlorine gas."

Spock said, "Most interesting. Why chlorine, Mr. Sulu?"

Sulu looked at him. "I checked with the chief engineer. He has the materials to manufacture a sufficient quantity of chlorine. Also, it's heavier than air. It will sink into every crevice on board."

Ensign Chekov snorted, "It isn't bad enough that we're threatened first with space cafard and then with bubonic plague. Now Sulu wants to gas us."

"That will be all, Mr. Chekov," the captain said curtly. And then to Sulu, "Let's have the rest of it."

"Sir," Sulu said doggedly, "the whole crew can be put in space suits and remain in them for three hours. In that time we can fill the ship with gas. Nobody knows where Mickey's managed to hide himself, but, wherever it is, the gas will get him. After three hours we can blow the ship clean with the ventilating system and it will be safe to discard the space suits."

Kirk looked at Spock. "Comments, Mr. Spock?"

Spock's face was thoughtful. "Captain, it seems fairly reasonable to me. Not only, ah, Mickey, but any rat fleas he carries would be susceptible to chlorine, a most deadly gas of the halogen family, once used in warfare. And, as you know, our other alternatives are rapidly disappearing. Neither Dr. McCoy nor I has been able to locate anything in our library banks that would help us fight the disease."

"Which amazes me," Kirk muttered.

"Not at all, Captain. We can find historical references to bubonic plague, but, as the doctor has pointed out, there is no call for a description of the black death and its cure to be on file. It has long since been conquered and is now medically unknown."

Kirk turned again to Sulu. "Very well, Mr. Sulu. Make the necessary arrangements. You have my go-ahead."

So they donned their space suits, the intrepid personnel of the pride of the Starfleet, the U.S.S. *Enterprise,* and they deluged their ship with the deadly green gas. They saturated it. They let the gas soak into every corner and crevice for three full hours; then they blew the ship clear.

When officers and crew climbed from their suits, all over the vessel, they looked sheepishly at each other. It had been a long fight, and they had won, but somehow they weren't proud of the victory. They knew that somewhere, in his remote hiding place, Mickey was dead, but they found little satisfaction in the fact. It was as though a respected adversary had been conquered, and conquered by superior weight of numbers, by trickery, by double-dealing, not by honest warfare.

A toast was drunk to Mickey's passing in the captain's quarters, and similar ones through the junior officers', noncommissioned officers', and enlisted men's messes. All listened respectfully when Lieutenant Uhura sang over the intercom the last stanza of "The Saga of Mickey the Space Rat."

Which should be the end of the story of Mickey—but isn't.

With the passing of Operation Mickey, the ship drifted back into its routine and, in a week's time, except for the occasional nostalgic conversations about Mickey, the little rodent was forgotten. Lethargy was again the word, and the monotony of space travel

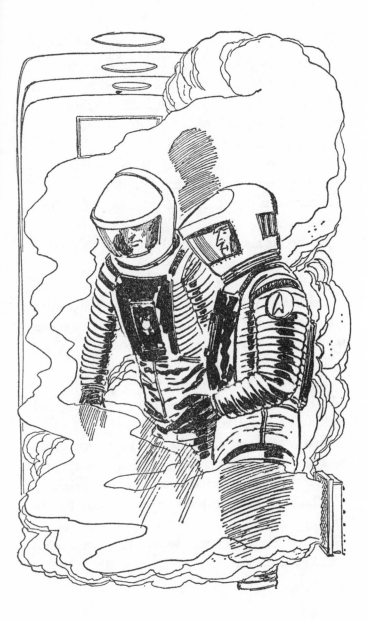

once again flung its drab coat over the *Enterprise*.

Between watches Captain James Kirk drifted one day into the sick bay. His eyes went about the three-room complex, noting unhappily that all the beds in the sick bay proper were occupied.

Dr. McCoy straightened up from the electronic microscope over which he had been bent.

Kirk motioned with his head at the men in the beds. "Stasis again?"

The doctor nodded wordlessly.

"As many as before?"

"There soon will be."

Kirk said, "We're only a month out. You'd think that the prospect of the mission finally being over would hold them."

"It's been too long, Jim. Much too long."

"You think we'll make it?"

"I don't know. One bad case to start it rolling and we'll have had it, Jim."

There was a roar from the corridor beyond. Both Kirk and the doctor spun, eyes wide in dismay. Was this the all-out case of cafard they had been dreading?

"What's that?" the captain rasped, heading for the door.

The shouting continued, and now they could begin to make out the words.

"Mickey! *Mickey!*"

At the door Kirk exclaimed, "They've gone off their rockers!"

The doctor was immediately behind him.

Yeoman Janice Rand came hurrying up, her face flushed with excitement. "Captain! It's Mickey. They saw Mickey again, down in the ship's chapel. He's alive! Mickey's *still alive!*"

"Don't be ridiculous!"

But she was gone, darting down the corridor toward the sounds of excitement.

The captain looked at Dr. McCoy, his mouth slightly open.

"But he *couldn't* be alive."

It was all-out warfare now. Before, the campaign against Mickey had been pursued coldly, carefully, and without passion. The rat had been a potential danger, a threat to the whole ship, and was to be destroyed ruthlessly. Even so, there had been considerable sympathy for the little rodent.

Now it was different. An emotional crisis seemed to seize upon every man and woman aboard. The time and interest of everyone, from ship's officers to messmen, were devoted to the finding and destruction of Mickey. Groups, pairs, and solitary hunters roamed the ship at all hours, haggard and red-eyed, but armed to the teeth and seeking the elusive diseased rat.

The situation was a deadly serious one now. They were nearing their destination and they needed desperately to land, to escape the confinement of the starship. They needed to see their families, their wives, their sweethearts. They longed to see blue sky above them, to sprawl on beaches, swim in the sea, hike the countryside, ride, climb, run free of all limitations on space. The very thought of being confined indefinitely under quarantine against bubonic plague drove them to frenzy.

Mickey was flushed thrice in the first week. He escaped desperately each time, the roars of the hunters behind him.

In the second week of the wild hunt for him he was knocked down by half a dozen phasers on stun effect when he ventured into an ambush in storage compartment eight. He was quickly rushed to the ship's waste matter converter. The men who had approached and handled him were rushed to the sick bay for immediate decontamination.

Somehow it didn't seem real. It didn't seem possible that Mickey could be dead. Like the lives of his legendary foe, the cat, Mickey the Rat's lives had seemed all but endless.

That night Lieutenant Uhura was compelled by celebrating shipmates to write a final stanza to her saga, but when she took up her guitar to sing it, one of the two strings remaining went *ping*.

She made a woeful face in disgust.

"One string left," she said. "Well. . . ." She stood up, folded her arms, and began doing a takeoff on the shuffling walk of a Chinese woman playing a single-stringed instrument.

Lieutenant Chang, laughing, said, "This is *too* much. We've got to get back now, if only to buy new strings for Uhura's guitar."

AFTERMATH

THEY WERE within hours of star base touchdown.

Captain James Kirk sauntered along the ship's corridors, his face thoughtful. He reached the quarters of his first officer and knocked. When Spock's voice answered, he pushed his way in, still meditative.

Dr. McCoy was seated there. Obviously he and Spock had been in deep conversation.

The Vulcan came to his feet. "Ah, Captain. Are we soon to go into orbit?"

"A couple of hours or so, Mr. Spock." The captain looked at Dr. McCoy. "I figured out where Mickey was hiding," he said.

Mr. Spock's eyebrows went up. But Dr. McCoy said, "Oh? I thought you might. How?"

"Several little items that didn't quite jibe. For instance, supposedly plague has been unknown on Federation worlds for centuries, but it was on a Federation planet that Sulu acquired Mickey. Then, too, if the animal had the disease, how did he live aboard for so many months? Why didn't he die of it? And the way Mickey kept turning up just at the crucial time, when you needed something to get the crew's minds off their frustrations."

Kirk turned his eyes to Spock. "It never occurred to me to doubt your word when you said there was nothing in the ship's library computer banks on the cure for bubonic plague. Of course there was. Those banks contain all the information compiled by man down through the ages, including how to cure diseases now forgotten. But, of course, if Bones was to pull off his scheme and keep the crew's mind off cafard, he had to have your cooperation."

Spock said mildly, "A very interesting predicament, this danger of space cafard. I was happy to work with the doctor."

Kirk looked back at Dr. McCoy. "Where did you have him hidden? In the sick bay?"

"Most of the time." The doctor nodded. "When the ship was being gassed, I had him in an oxygen tent. While Sulu was searching the sick bay compartments, I had him tucked inside my tunic."

"You must have had a bit of trouble teaching him how to dance."

"A bit. Something to occupy my off-hours." McCoy twisted his face wryly. "Even a doctor is subject to cafard if he gets bored enough."

Captain James Kirk looked at the two of them wryly. "I suppose I should have something to say about discipline, and about a starship captain being hoodwinked by his first officer and ship's surgeon. However, I can't think of anything." He turned to go.

Dr. McCoy said, "One thing, Captain."

Kirk half-turned. "Yes?"

"Jim, *please* don't allow us to get into this spot again. I don't know *how* I'd ever keep cafard from hitting the ship next time."

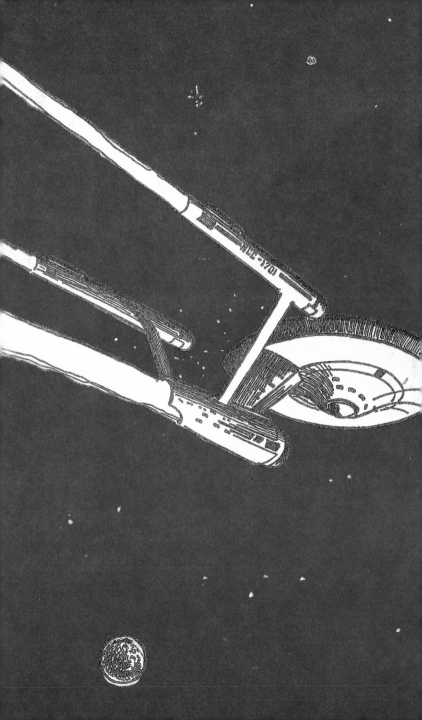